THE LEGACY OF THE LOST KEY

THE GRAIN OF SAND

ANISH

Contents

Prologue

Let me tell you about Adam and Emma, two extraordinary siblings whose adventures date back to May 2003.

Introducing Adam Wilson, a gifted fourteen-year-old wonder whose intellectual ability shines brilliantly amongst the complex puzzles of life.

It is a well-known fact that Adam possesses an uncanny ability to decipher riddles with astonishing ease. Present him with a riddle, and you will witness the marvel of his intellect as he delivers the correct answer on his very first attempt. Not just that, Adam possesses the ability to use an enigma, an encrypted mode of communication used during WW1. Yeah, you heard me right. Imagine a teenage codebreaker, and you've got Adam in a nutshell.

But within that brilliant brain of his, there was a catch. Sometimes, his memory would play hide and seek with him. It's like having a supercomputer with an occasional glitch. But hey, that just added an element of surprise to their adventures.

Then, there is Emma, his younger sister, a mere nine-year-old, yet possessing an extraordinary gift that defies her tender years.

Her characteristic survival capabilities are nothing short of awe-inspiring. She is a master of navigating labyrinths, too.

Emma's resourcefulness is legendary; she has the remarkable ability to transmute commonplace objects into extraordinary tools, a talent that often proves indispensable on their adventures. You know those moments when you're stuck in a specific problem and you're like, 'If only I had this *thing* to solve the problem'? Emma's the one who would whip up that *thing* from thin air.

In the narrative that unfolds, you will come to know Adam and Emma as two extraordinary siblings.

Their extraordinary abilities will lead them to confront the greatest mystery of all. (I will tell you what it is later.)

Chapter 1
The Mysterious Letter

Adam and Emma were enjoying their vacation.

They were in the middle of a game of chess. Yeah, you heard me right, chess! These two were all about the intellectual game of strategy. Their faces were full of determination and hope.

Adam completely forgot the rules at one point and tried to move his bishop like a knight. Emma couldn't help but burst into a fit of laughter, nearly tipping over her chair. 'Oh, Adam, you can't just make up your own moves!'

But Adam, never one to be outdone, quickly recovered from his blunder. With a twinkle in his eye, he retorted, 'Well, maybe I'm just inventing a new style of chess! You know, "Freestyle Chess," where I can move my bishop like a disco dancer.'

Their game continued. Each move was more outrageous than the last.

Adam had just executed a brilliant move and declared, 'Checkmate!'

Emma let out a sigh of frustration, her brow furrowing.

'I still don't get it. Why do *you* always win?'

Adam offered a reassuring smile.

'It's all about that good old strategy, Emma. You'll figure it out with practice. Better luck next time.'

'You always say that! You'll know what your so-called "strategy" is when *I* defeat you.'

Emma snapped, throwing her hands up in frustration before storming out of the room. Her enthusiasm diminished. Who knew that just a single move could turn enthusiasm into frustration?

Adam and Emma usually play chess. It's one of their many hobbies. They do love to play chess. That's what they do when they're chillin' out. But, every time they play, Adam's the one to win until Adam is kind enough to let Emma win, which... does happen, unlike what you might think.

Yet Emma has determination. Even though she lost every single time, she never quit playing with Adam. After all, that's the only thing she can do all day, as she has no interest in anything outdoors unless something like this happens.

As Emma left, storming out of the room, her curiosity led her to wander into Professor Mitchell Wilson's study. Wait. You don't know who Professor Mitchell Wilson is, do you? Let me tell you who he is.

Well, Adam and Emma had grown up as the children of two well-educated parents who were renowned archaeologists known for their daring expeditions. Yeah! Expeditions.

From an early age, the siblings immersed themselves in the world of ancient artifacts, lost civilizations, and unsolved mysteries. In their free time, their parents used to work on a secret mission, which remains concealed from Adam and Emma. And you won't believe how they love history.

Then came the day their parents left for what they had casually referred to as a quick trip to the store, promising to return shortly after buying some milk. Yet they never did. Adam was just seven years old at that time, and Emma was a mere two-year-old toddler!

They obviously needed a new guardian, right? Professor Mitchell, their uncle, stepped in to care for them, providing guidance and stability.

However, Professor Mitchell eventually accepted a job in Italy, far from their American home. Now, it was the Professor's wife, Mary Wilson, who took on the role of guardian until now.

The siblings' aunt, Mary Wilson, is seriously one of the kindest souls out there. I mean, this lady is always ready to lend a hand and knows how to handle anything life throws at her. And let me tell you, she's like a box full of talents. (I'll speak about her talents later in this very narrative.)

But above all, it is her exceptional ability for reasoning and logical thinking that genuinely distinguishes her. Believe me, when confronted with the irrational or nonsensical, Aunt Mary's tolerance is swiftly depleted. But here's the kicker: get her into a good old logical chat, and she loses track of time faster than you'll know. She is wild. (You'll know why later.)

Now, coming back to Emma.

As Emma left, storming out of the room, her curiosity led her to wander into Professor Mitchell Wilson's study, a room filled with an atmosphere of history and secrets. It was a place where the air seemed to whisper tales of ancient civilizations and hidden knowledge. And on that fateful day, something caught Emma's eye—drops of ink splattered across an old parchment. Yeah, and by old parchment, I really mean *old* parchment.

'What's that?' Emma said to herself.

Emma was aware that Professor Mitchell was in Italy for work, leaving no room for his involvement in the spilled ink. Furthermore, the vision of anyone entering Professor Mitchell's room was unthinkable. Yet Emma was determined in her quest for answers.

With determination coursing through her veins, she pushed herself into the professor's study, stepping into a chamber she had never entered before. It was her first time ever experiencing the vintage feel of Professor Mitchell's room. For you, let's just say it was like stepping on the moon for the first time.

The parchment, lying on the Professor's workstation, had markings covered by the ink's possibly accidental splatter. Yes, accidental. That's because no one would ever want to come and splatter ink on purpose, right? That too in Professor Mitchell's room.

And the ink? Well, it had a very unusual odor. Not something that regular ink would smell like. The distinctive odor of the ink reminded her of her school's chemistry lab. The smell of the ink spread across the room, adding another layer of intrigue to the puzzle.

As she peered closer, Emma discovered that there were symbols and pictures on the parchment. Not words. It was something altogether unfamiliar.

Astonishment washed over her as she grasped what she had stumbled upon. Realizing that she couldn't solve this mystery alone, she hastily made her way to her brother, Adam, eager to share her discovery.

'Hey, Adam! You won't believe what I found in Uncle Mitchell's study!' said Emma, running into their room and almost tripping over a chess piece.

'Whoa, slow down, Emma!' Adam replied with a smile, setting aside the chessboard. 'What did you find? Another ancient puzzle to solve?'

Emma's eyes sparkled with excitement as she launched into her tale.

'It's something even more mysterious, Adam. Come see for yourself!'

She tugged at his arm, urging him to follow her.

Adam, always eager for a new adventure, couldn't resist his sister's enthusiasm. He took a notebook and pen and finally said,

'Alright, all right, lead the way, Sherlock. Let's see what you've got.'

Emma took her brother with a nice little smile on her face. And yeah, she totally forgot that she had lost a chess match.

'Look! This is what I found.'

'That's great, and how did you find it? You did not storm into the room, did you?'

'No, why would I? I saw this while I was walking by the corridor.' Emma said.

'Walking? You weren't walking. You were *angry* at me and stormed out of the room.' Adam corrected her.

'Whatever.' Emma was frustrated again. Adam had reminded her of the chess match she lost. But let the past be in the past. Let's come back to the present.

'Now, let me see the parchment,' Adam said as he looked at the parchment.

At first, Adam hesitated to pick up the parchment, but how do you think he would be able to resist picking up the parchment? He picked it up.

'I don't think that those are words,' Emma mentioned, pointing at the script on the parchment.

Adam examined the markings and the partially obscured text, his eyes narrowing in concentration.

'These *are* words, Emma.'

'How?'

'Each symbol represents a phonetic sound. But this is obviously not a modern language. It's some sort of ancient script, possibly from a bygone civilization.'

'Never knew pictures could make words.'

'And... did you find anything else?'

'Yeah. The ink–did you smell the ink? It smells like our chemistry lab at school.'

'Chemistry lab?'

'Yeah. Chemistry lab'

'Well, to me, it smells like some kind of... fruit.'

'Fruit? How is this... Wait, it smells like... pomegranate.'

'Right! That's what I meant.' Adam exclaimed.

'But it does smell like some acid.'

'Hmm... It smells like rusted iron, but we can focus on the text for now.'

'Text?'

'Yeah? What's wrong with it?'

'Nothing's wrong, but how on earth are *we* supposed to know what this language is? Do you think we stand a chance at understanding it?' Emma spoke in a cacophonous voice. Her voice held a mix of curiosity and doubt as she gazed at the script before them.

'Easy, Emma. Keep your voice down. We don't want Aunt to hear us.'

'All right! I'll be quiet.' Emma replied in a hushed tone.

'You know, Emma, this script looks like the Ancient Egyptian hieroglyphs.'

'How are you *so* sure?'

'Well, it could also be other hieroglyphs. I don't have all the details since it's not something I've studied in detail, but I remember Dad mentioning it once when I asked him about Ancient Egyptian scripts.'

'Then how do we decode it?

'I remember that he mentioned how a person named Jean-François Champollion decoded the hieroglyphs. He also told me how to decode a hieroglyph, but... I forgot.'

'Why are you so forgetful? If you had remembered how to decode it, our work would have been easier!' Emma shouted at Adam.

'Cool down.'

'I wish Dad would have told *me* about it.'

'You weren't born by then.' As Adam said so, Emma's face was like, 'Duh! Why was I not the elder one?'

Adam reached for the notebook and pen.

'I think I'll rewrite the script we can see here.' He said.

'Yeah. It might be a starting point for further research on Egyptian hieroglyphs.'

Adam starts copying the script as Emma watches him do so.

He ends up writing down something that looks like this:

Weird? I know that you have no idea what this means, but don't worry. Our buddies, Adam and Emma, will decode it for you. All you have to do is sit tight and read on.

'Good thing I'm good at art.' Adam started. 'It looks like there are three words. I hope we can find some source for knowing more about this hieroglyph.' Adam said with hope. 'What do you think?'

'I think it's time to leave,' Emma said with a short laugh.

'Not the answer I expected...' Adam smiled. '...but yeah. We must leave.'

As Adam and Emma quietly exited the room, they came across an unexpected sight.

Aunt Mary stood at the door, her expression a mix of surprise and concern.

Caught in the act, the siblings exchanged nervous glances, their hearts racing as they wondered how much she might have overheard.

'Uh... What are you doing here?' Adam asked Aunt Mary as he stuttered.

'You're asking what I'm doing here? It feels like the question should be, what are *you two* doing here?'

Her tone conveyed a sense of suspicion, leaving Adam and Emma aware that their secret discovery might not remain a secret for long.

'Umm... We discovered that some ink was spilled in uncle's room, so...' Yeah. Adam was trying to make up a story, but he was interrupted by Emma.

'Actually, Aunt Mary,' she began hesitantly, 'we were just exploring around, and we stumbled upon something in Uncle's study. It's... It's something strange, something we don't quite understand yet.'

Her voice quivered slightly, conveying a sense of nervousness.

Adam nodded in agreement.

'Yes, that's right. We were just curious, and we didn't mean to intrude. We were about to come and tell you.'

Emma glared at Adam, as they were not actually planning to tell Aunt Mary about it.

'Oh... So, what is it that you discovered? Is it something about your uncle?' Aunt Mary asked with curiosity.

Aunt Mary's curiosity and interest in the topic were surprising.

The siblings expected Aunt Mary to scold them or something, but that didn't happen. She seemed to praise and encourage them for their discovery indirectly. Good old Aunt Mary!

'It's not related to Uncle Mitchell, as far as we can tell,' Adam began, 'but it's something uncommon to be found in his room. Come and see for yourself.'

Aunt Mary entered the room. And as she saw the spilled ink, she said, 'You didn't spill it, did you?'

'Obviously not. Why would we?' Adam said.

'Okay, but how did you find it?'

'I was just walking–' Emma started.

'You weren't walking–' Adam interrupted. He couldn't help but tease her.

'Argh... fine. I stormed out of the room...' Emma corrected herself, '...after losing the chess match. And then, I stumbled upon the spilled ink.'

And then Aunt Mary was like, 'Uh, huh? What made you come in?' Emma felt a bit irritated with

Aunt Mary asking a lot of questions. I don't know about you, but Emma couldn't tell whether Aunt Mary was about to scold them or not.

'When I saw it, I came in to... I don't know why I came in.'

'You were curious, right?' Adam asked.

'Yeah. I was just curious. Then I saw the parchment on the table.' Emma said, agreeing with Adam's point.

'What about the rest of our discovery?' Adam asked.

'Right! I found out that the ink on the parchment smelled like our chemistry lab. Adam said that it smells like pomegranate and iron.'

Aunt Mary smelled the ink. 'You're right. This smells like rusted iron and a bit like pomegranate, too.'

'Also, the script on the parchment is probably Egyptian hieroglyphs. And again, I do not know for sure.'

'I must say,' Aunt Mary remarked with astonishment, 'you two have the makings of a great detective.'

'More like untrained historians and archaeologists,' Adam said.

'May I ask why?'

'This writing here can only be deciphered by someone who knows the Ancient Egyptian hieroglyphs. This is something that we may not be able to decode easily. It could be anything. As far as I know, I can say that three different words are waiting for us to decode them.' Adam mentioned desperately.

'We will find out what it says,' Emma said with determination.

Aunt Mary nodded, her pride in their curiosity and determination evident.

'I have a feeling you two are onto something fascinating. Please let me know when you uncover the meaning behind those ancient symbols. I'm genuinely interested in this mystery.' Yeah. You read it right. Aunt Mary didn't scold them but... praised them.

Aunt Mary had been a part of their lives ever since Adam and Emma could remember.

She was their mother's younger sister, and while they had known her throughout their childhood, it was only after their parents' disappearance that Aunt Mary had become their guardian. Adam and Emma had become her responsibility, and she was determined to ensure that they were not just cared for but also educated in ways beyond ordinary schooling.

With Aunt Mary's unexpected support and encouragement, the siblings felt even more determined to unlock the secrets of the hieroglyph. Their shared journey into the unknown had just gained a new ally. How wonderful!

Chapter 2
Valley of Knowledge

Emma was always very curious and eager to know more.

It could be about the past of the universe or the past of the world. It could also be the future. She is always curious, no matter what. She also has a knack for getting excited very quickly. I guess you already figured it out by now. And now, since her and Adam's discovery at Professor Mitchell's study, Emma's curiosity has reached its peak.

She had been searching all throughout the Professor's room for further clues or information on Ancient Egyptian hieroglyphs. It was something she had never done.

But Adam was the calm one. He was literally chillin' out like nothing ever happened. It's like he didn't even know anything about the discovery. The siblings are just not connected through characteristics, right?

Emma, who had been searching for hours, found details of several books about Egyptian architecture. She also found a book that contained Egyptian Mythology. Well and good. But she had no luck finding a book containing information about Egyptian hieroglyphs.

Adam thought to check up on her. He wanted to see what she was doing. He kept the book he was reading down and wearily walked to Professor Mitchell's room.

'Any luck?' He asked Emma.

'No. All I found were some books about the architecture of Egypt. Nothing much.'

'What's this?' Adam picked up a book.'

'That? Oh, that's just Egyptian Mythology. There's nothing much to see.'

With that small discussion, Adam returned to the book he was reading. Right. Adam was just hangin' out with his book, and Emma was doing all the research work. Well, Emma did like doing the research, so I guess it doesn't matter.

At first, Emma thought that her search for clues would never end until...

'Adam! Come here. Quick,' Emma shouted with urgency.

Adam, who had been hanging out with his book in the other room, set aside the book he was reading and hurried to Emma's side.

'What is it?' he asked, concern etched across his face.

'Take a look at this, Adam. A map of Egypt,' she urged, and as usual, her excitement was clearly visible in her voice.

With a sparkle in her eyes, Emma unfolded a map before him.

Adam looked at the map and said, 'Wow! That's a great discovery.'

'I know, right?' Emma was happy, as Adam had complimented her discovery.

'And look at this,' Adam pointed to a text.

C percent accurate tabula Aegypti

If you don't understand it, don't worry. Adam and Emma will translate it for you.

'I think that it is Latin. "C" refers to hundred in Roman numerals, right?' Emma said with excitement.

'Yeah.' Adam saw where she was going.

'Then... 'C percent accurate' must mean hundred percent accurate.'

'Right!'

'What's tabula, then?'

'I think tabula means map,' Adam said, wondering whether his translation was correct.

'But what is Aegypti?' Emma wondered aloud.

'If I'm right, it must be Egypt. The Romans named Egypt Aegypti.' Adam said.

'So that means this is a hundred percent accurate map of Egypt.' Hundred percent accurate? Aren't all maps one hundred percent accurate?

'Yeah. If this is *really* a hundred percent accurate, then it could help us find out more about Egypt. We will have to inspect this map for a clue. I give this task to you.'

Emma has keen eyes, right? That would really help her with observation. But inspecting observations is something that Adam has a knack for. Well, keeping that in mind, Emma thought that she might not be able to discover much without Adam, but then... she changed her mind. She had lost that fateful chess match, and with it, a sense of frustration had welled up inside her.

She had promised to prove to Adam that she had her own 'strategies.' Emma's eyes met Adam's as he studied the map, and a silent resolve passed between them. She knew that this was her chance to show him that she could take the lead and that she was more than capable of navigating their way through this adventure.

'Sure! I'll investigate on this map.' Emma finally said.

'Great! Meanwhile, I'll read the book I was reading.' Saying so, Adam went back to chill out with his book.

One fateful evening, Emma found herself seated at the antique wooden table in their room.

Emma found herself in their cluttered room, surrounded by dusty books, scrolls, and probably a few stray socks because, let's be honest, whose room is ever spotless? Well, maybe, except for Aunt Mary's.

It was all the work of their parents, who decorated their room so beautifully before they left with no sign. It was the perfect place to begin her quest. A mystical quest must be accomplished at a place that feels historical. You've got to set the mood. So, the room's perfect, right?

In front of her lay the well-worn map of Egypt, its edges frayed and corners curled from years of use. It must have belonged to her parents and uncle, guiding them on their countless journeys.

Now, it was in Emma's hands–a treasure map of knowledge waiting to be deciphered. Yeah, you heard me right. A treasure map You'll know why later.

Her gaze swept over the map's intricate details, tracing the course of the Nile as it wound its way through the desert sands.

It obviously looked like it was a hundred percent accurate. She knew that somewhere within this ancient land lay the key to unlocking the secrets of the hieroglyph. Her fingers danced lightly over the paper. Yeah, I'm not kidding, 'danced'. She's a bit playful.

With a determined spark in her eyes, Emma focused on her task. She searched for any clues that might lead her to a place where she could learn about Egyptian hieroglyphs, the key to understanding the mysterious script on the parchment.

Her fingertip followed the river's course until it settled on a location marked 'The Valley of Knowledge.'

'The Valley of Knowledge!' she whispered to herself, as she couldn't contain her excitement.

Finding Adam engrossed in a book in their shared room, Emma burst in with enthusiasm.

'Adam! You won't believe what I've found!' Her voice rang with excitement and startled Adam.

Adam, the calm, collected, bookish older brother, raises an eyebrow, probably like, 'What's Emma up to now?'

Adam finally spoke up, 'What's got you so worked up, Emma?'

'Why don't you see for yourself?' Emma told Adam.

Adam kept his book down and went to look at Emma's discovery.

With a grin, Emma showed the map on the table in front of him, her finger pointing to the marked location. 'The Valley of Knowledge,' she declared.

'I think it might be the key to learning about Egyptian hieroglyphs.' She added on.

Adam's eyes widened as he examined the map and the marked location. He could see the possibilities stretching out before them.

'That's incredible, Emma. The Valley of Knowledge seems like the perfect place to find the knowledge that we need to decipher the hieroglyph.'

'Yeah. That's why I called you to see it.'

Adam was thinking, 'Wow, I've got one great sister. Hieroglyphs? Check. Ancient maps? Double check.'

'But how do we get there? It looks like a long journey.' Adam asked. His practical side kicked in.

Emma nodded. 'I've been thinking about that. We might need to plan carefully, gather supplies, and perhaps even find someone who knows the way. But

I'm willing to do whatever it takes to unravel this mystery. And you know what? Aunt Mary might just be the key to getting us there. She seems to be as eager as we are to decode the script and discover its secrets.'

The siblings realized that their quest was gaining momentum. Aunt Mary's assistance added a new layer of hope to their endeavor as they began to sketch out their plans, ready to embark on an adventure that would lead them into the heart of history itself.

'But then we have a problem,' Adam spoke up after thinking for a while. 'We can't be sure that The Valley of Knowledge will have the key to our discovery. What if we just go there and come back with nothing?' Adam was thinking about it. 'I don't wanna go there for nothing.' Pretty logical, right? Like, what's the use of going there if you come back with nothing?

Adam's words of caution hung in the air, a reminder of the uncertainty that shrouded their quest. If that happened to me, I'd be totally frustrated with spending money on nothing.

'You're right, Adam,' Emma admitted, her enthusiasm tempered by the practicality of his concerns. 'There are no guarantees that The Valley of Knowledge will hold the key to our discovery. But isn't that what makes it an adventure? The thrill of the unknown, the chance to uncover something extraordinary.' She said.

'Yeah. And you know what, Emma? At least we get to visit Egypt.' That's… a valid point.

Emma said with a short laugh. 'Yeah, you're right.' She paused, then added with a determined glint in her eye, 'And as for Aunt Mary, let's approach her with our plan. She's been supportive so far, and if she's willing to take us to Egypt, it could be the first step in our journey.

'You're right. Although Aunt Mary's help was unexpected, she could be a great part of our quest.' Adam said.

With undiminished determination, the siblings agreed to seek Aunt Mary's guidance and hoped that 'The Valley of Knowledge' would indeed hold the answers they sought.

They knew that the path ahead was uncertain, but they were ready to embrace the adventure, whatever it might bring.

With their plans in place and hope in their hearts, Adam and Emma made their way to find Aunt Mary. Let's see whether she agrees or not.

They found her sitting on a chair in the living room. They were surprised to see her with the parchment that they had discovered. She seemed to be trying to understand what was written on it, although she knew that it'd require a whole lot of expertise to decode it.

'Aunt Mary,' Emma began, her voice filled with a mix of excitement and seriousness, 'we have something important to talk to you about.'

Aunt Mary looked up from the parchment, her gaze shifting between the siblings.

'Of course, what is it, dear?' She asked, her gentle behavior putting them at ease.

Adam took a step forward, ready to explain their newfound quest.

'We've discovered something fascinating, something that could help us understand the mysterious script that you are holding right now. We believe it might lead us to a place where we can learn what's written on the parchment.'

Emma continued, 'We were wondering if you'd be willing to take us to Egypt. It's a big ask, we know, but we feel this is a once-in-a-lifetime opportunity.'

Aunt Mary listened attentively, her eyes reflecting their enthusiasm. After a thoughtful pause, she smiled warmly and said,

'I can see the passion and determination in both of you. If this is something that could help you unravel this strange mystery, then I'm more than willing to support you on this journey.'

That was an unexpected answer. I mean, she literally agreed on one shot! Tears of gratitude welled up in Emma's eyes, and Adam couldn't help but feel a rush of excitement.

'Aunt Mary has made our work much easier, right?' Emma said.

'Yeah, without her, we wouldn't even be able to hope for decoding the text.'

With Aunt Mary's support, their dream of exploring 'The Valley of Knowledge' and decoding the ancient hieroglyph was one step closer to becoming a reality.

With Aunt Mary's encouragement, they started planning their trip.

'We'll need to make arrangements for our stay in Egypt and figure out the plan,' Adam said, grabbing a notebook and pen.

Aunt Mary nodded. 'I can help you with that. We want to ensure you have everything you need for your research.'

Together, they began to discuss their upcoming adventure, eager to go on a journey that would take them to Egypt's history and secrets.

'Aunt Mary, we can't thank you enough for your support in this adventure. It means the world to us.' Emma said.

'Absolutely. But first, we should look into travel arrangements. Flights to Egypt, visas, and accommodations.'

'I can handle the flight and visa arrangements.' Aunt Amry said.

'Perfect, that's one less thing to worry about. We also need to consider our supplies and equipment for research.' Emma said.

'I can help you with that as well. We'll need some specialized equipment for hieroglyphic research, such as a geological hammer, notebooks, and perhaps even some chemical analysis tools.'

'Thank you so much, Aunt Mary. We're incredibly grateful for your support and guidance.'

'You're both passionate about this, and I believe in your potential. Let's make sure we're fully prepared for this adventure. Once we have all the details leveled out, we can start planning the journey itself.'

Aunt Mary was determined to support Adam and Emma's quest to unravel the mysteries of the hieratic script and explore 'The Valley of Knowledge' in Egypt. With her firm commitment to their journey, she decided to take a significant step to make their dream a reality.

Over the next few days, Aunt Mary worked tirelessly to arrange a private flight to Egypt for the siblings.

She knew that this adventure held great significance for them, connecting them to their family's legacy and satisfying their hunger for knowledge. How grateful they must be to Aunt Mary! This very soul is the kindest of all the people I've ever met!

Finally, the day of departure arrived. The siblings, filled with expectation and excitement, boarded the private plane that Aunt Mary had secured for them. Yeah. When you have Aunt Mary, forget about those regular planes. You'll literally get a private plane! I mean, who needs a commercial when you can have your own plane, right?

They packed several snacks for them, as it was a long journey. As they buckled their seatbelts and looked out at the endless sky, they knew they were embarking on an adventure of a lifetime, one that would take them to the heart of Egypt's history and mysteries.

On the plane, as they buckled their seatbelts and prepared for takeoff, Emma turned to Adam with her face lit up with expectancy. 'Can you believe we're actually doing this? Our dream of exploring 'The Valley of Knowledge' is finally coming true!'

I don't know about you, but I can say that what Adam and Emma were genuinely excited about was not deciphering the hieroglyph. But it was going to Egypt. In fact, it was their first time ever going out of America.

With Aunt Mary's support and the promise of new discoveries ahead, Adam and Emma's journey had truly begun, and they were ready to embrace the unknown.

Emma turns to Adam, her face filled with eagerness. She's all about the adventure, and so are we, right? So, fasten your seatbelts because things are about to get wild and hieroglyphic. Beware!

Chapter 3
Off to Egypt

Did you read the chapter title? We're off to Egypt!

Excitement filled the air as the plane was about to take off. But here's the catch: They start noticing something fishy. And no, it's not a Nile catfish or a Nile tigerfish. Adam and Emma began to exchange curious glances.

Emma, the voice of curiosity, goes, 'Hey, where's the pilot?' Yeah, you heard it right. No pilot! I mean, you can't blame her. Planes tend to work better with someone steering the ship, right?

Adam, too, noticed that there was no pilot.

'I have no idea. How do you think I'll know where the pilot is?' he replied, his brows furrowing in concern.

After a minute or so, Adam spoke up.

'And come to think of it, where's Aunt Mary? She's not on the plane either,' Adam said. So, just to clarify, they're on a plane, but there's no pilot and no Aunt Mary. Yeah, I know what you're thinking, and it's just as wild as it sounds.

'Right! Where could Aunt Mary be?' Emma, too, noticed that Aunt Mary wasn't there.

As the realization dawned upon them that there were no visible pilots or crew members, a sense of unease settled in. They exchanged worried looks, wondering if there had been some kind of mix-up or miscommunication. They wanted to call Aunt Mary, but they couldn't. After all, Aunt Mary was the only one with a good old Nokia. Don't judge them; it's 2003.

Just as their concern was reaching its peak, Aunt Mary's voice came over the intercom, filling the cabin with a reassuring tone.

'Don't worry, you two. Everything is under control.'

Both Adam and Emma let out a sigh of relief at the sound of her voice. But their curiosity got the better of them, and Adam couldn't help but wonder aloud.

Adam, who's probably still trying to figure out the plane's emergency exit locations, goes, 'Aunt Mary, where are you? And who's flying the plane?'

There was a soft chuckle in Aunt Mary's response.

'Well, I'm sorry, as I realize that I should have mentioned this earlier, but I happen to have a pilot's license. You see, before marriage, I used to work as a pilot. I'll be your captain for this flight.'

Yes, Aunt Mary has a pilot's license! And no one saw that one coming, not even the plane! The siblings exchanged astonished glances, their surprise quickly giving way to admiration for their resourceful and multi-talented aunt. After all, it's the resourceful Aunt Mary who has a knack for several things.

'I never knew Aunt Mary had a pilot's license!' Emma said.

'Neither did I.'

As the plane continued its journey towards Egypt, they settled into their seats, ready to experience the adventure ahead.

Their adventure reminded them of their childhood, when they used to believe in fantasy and fiction tales. To them, the journey was like something out of a fictional story. Mysteries and riddles were all that they could think about.

As the plane sped down the runway and gracefully lifted off the ground, Adam and Emma watched as their homeland disappeared beneath the clouds.

The sensation of flight filled them with excitement, and they gazed out the windows at the changing landscape below.

During the flight, they enjoyed the snacks they had packed, savoring the taste of their adventure with every bite.

As they soared through the sky, they shared their thoughts and dreams about what lay ahead.

Emma leaned over to Adam and said, 'Can you believe we're actually on our way to Egypt? I mean, it was just a dream a few days ago.'

Adam grinned and replied, 'I know, it's incredible. I can't wait to see The Valley of Knowledge and explore ancient Egyptian hieroglyphs.'

Emma nodded eagerly. Her eyes were sparkling. 'And to think, all of this started with a spilled ink stain on parchment. Life is full of surprises.'

Adam chuckled and added, 'And we have Aunt Mary to thank for making it all possible. She's quite the pilot, isn't she?'

Emma nodded, 'Definitely. She's been so supportive and encouraging. We're lucky to have her on our side.'

Their conversation continued, filled with excitement and expectation, as they looked forward to the adventures and discoveries that awaited them in Egypt.

The hours in the air passed by quickly as they admired the scenery, from vast deserts to winding rivers and bustling cities. They couldn't help but feel a sense of wonder as they voyaged closer to Egypt, a land steeped in history and mystery. Oh! It rhymes

Adam and Emma felt a flow of hope. As they peered out the window, the land of Egypt came into view, with its iconic pyramids and the winding Nile River. They had arrived at their destination, ready for a journey that would (probably) take them deeper into the heart of the past.

They stared at the Pyramids and the Nile like it was the most incredible show on Earth. To be honest, it probably is! But hey, it's 2003, so they're not taking selfies, but they're soaking in the view.

With a gentle touchdown, the plane glided smoothly to a stop at Cairo International Airport.

As the engines powered down, Adam and Emma could hardly contain their excitement.

Eagerly, they unfastened their seatbelts and made their way to the exit. Stepping off the plane and onto the land, they were greeted by the warm Egyptian sun and the bustling atmosphere of the airport.

Their hearts raced with eagerness as they took their first steps on Egyptian soil. The sights, sounds, and scents of this ancient land filled the air, and they knew that their adventure had truly begun.

'This is our first, and maybe the last, time in Egypt,' Emma said.

'You're right, Emma. Who knows who would have brought us to Egypt for no reason.' Adam said with a smile.

With every passing moment, they were drawn closer to 'The Valley of Knowledge' and the mysteries that awaited them there. Adam and Emma couldn't help but exchange excited glances, ready to immerse themselves in the history, culture, and secrets of Egypt.

But there's a little hitch. Aunt Mary has no idea where they're actually supposed to go.

'I just realized something,' Emma said.

'What?'

'Aunt Mary doesn't even know where we have to go.'

'You did not tell her about 'The Valley of Knowledge'?'

'No...'

Emma took out the map. She located the Valley of Knowledge. It was located to the east of the northernmost part of the delta of the Nile, near Alexandria. She handed it over to Aunt Mary.

'Aunt Mary, this is where we have to go. It's not so far from here. We could take a taxi or something to Alexandria.' Emma said.

'Hmm... So that's where you have to go. The Valley of Knowledge, huh? Interesting. I'll quickly find a taxi. You two stay here.' Aunt Mary replied with curiosity and eagerness.

She looked around the airport and found a taxi.

'Will you take us to Alexandria?' Aunt Mary asked the taxi driver.

'Sure, but where exactly in Alexandria?'

'The Valley of Knowledge.' But guess what? The taxi driver doesn't seem to know about The Valley of Knowledge. He was like, 'Huh? Never heard of that place.'

'It's here.' Aunt Mary pointed to The Valley of Knowledge on the map and showed it to the taxi driver.

'I can take you there, but I can assure you that there is nothing over there. It's just flat desert.'

Aunt Mary didn't care and called upon Adam and Emma. 'Guys! Come here. I found a taxi.'

'Great!' Adam said

As they got into the taxi, Aunt Mary spoke up.

'According to the taxi driver, there is nothing called The Valley of Knowledge.'

Adam and Emma exchanged puzzled glances as they settled into the taxi, their excitement giving way to a sense of confusion. Aunt Mary's disclosure that there was supposedly no place known as The Valley of Knowledge left them momentarily taken aback.

Adam leaned forward, addressing the taxi driver with a mix of curiosity and concern.

'Are you sure, sir? We've heard about this place, and we were hoping to visit it. It's related to a unique adventure we're on.'

The taxi driver, an old man with a friendly character, glanced at them through the rearview mirror.

'I understand your enthusiasm, but I've been driving in this region for years, and I've never heard of such a place. It could be a misunderstanding or perhaps a local legend.'

Aunt Mary chimed in, 'Thank you for your input. We'll continue on our journey and see what we can find. Maybe we'll come across someone who can point us in the right direction.'

With a sense of determination, they continued their drive through the desert. The mystery of The Valley of Knowledge was persistent in the air. As they went deeper into the arid landscape, they couldn't help but wonder if they were chasing a mirage or if there was a hidden truth waiting to be uncovered.

'What if the taxi driver is right?' Emma said

'I don't know. We might just be chasing a mirage in the middle of this sandy oven.' Adam said. You know, he's dropping some deep thoughts right there in the scorching desert heat.

The taxi rumbled along the desert highway, leaving the bustling city of Cairo behind. The endless expanse of golden sand stretched out before them, interrupted only by the occasional cluster of palm trees.

Inside the taxi, Adam, Emma, and Aunt Mary were engaged in a quiet discussion, trying to make sense of their journey.

'We're getting close,' Aunt Mary murmured, her eyes scanning the horizon.

'Right. I have a feeling that The Valley of Knowledge is somewhere out there.' Adam said

Emma nodded in agreement. Her gaze fixed on the shifting dunes.

'We can't give up now. We've come too far to turn back.' She spoke.

As they drove deeper into the desert, the landscape grew more remote and isolated. The taxi driver's confusion was evident as he continued to insist that there was no such place as The Valley of Knowledge.

Aunt Mary glanced at Adam and Emma. Her expression was filled with determination.

'I still don't think there's anything there.' The taxi driver said.

'We have to trust our instincts and the connection we feel to this place. It might not be visible to everyone, but we know it's real.' Aunt Mary spoke.

The taxi drove its way through the endless sands, and the siblings couldn't help but feel a growing sense of anticipation.

The Valley of Knowledge was waiting, hidden from the world but beckoning to them with the promise of ancient wisdom.

As the sun dipped below the horizon, casting long shadows across the desert, a surreal sight appeared before them.

And then, there it is, in the middle of the desert. To Adam, Emma, and Aunt Mary, the landscape transformed into an oasis of verdant green, nestled within the protective embrace of towering sandstone cliffs. There they are, cruising through the desert, and boom! What do they see? A huge, huge, HUGE pyramid. If you don't understand how huge it is, let's just say that it was way taller than the Burj Khalifa. Wait, the Burj Khalifa's too tiny. Let's say that it was almost the height of Mount Everest. Great. Now you understand how huge it was?

'We've found it!' Emma exclaimed.

Aunt Mary nodded in agreement, her eyes shimmering with pride and wonder. 'The Valley of Knowledge.'

'This is the key to the mystery. This place is, like... super unique.'

'What's so unique, Adam?' Emma asked.

'Well, it's got greenery in the middle of the desert! Like, seriously, that's like finding a unicorn at a horse farm! Don't you see it?' Adam softly exclaimed.

'Yeah. Now that you said it, I see the uniqueness.'

They had arrived, standing on the edge of a place hidden from the world, a place where all secrets and wisdom are stored.

But as they marveled at the sight, they noticed the taxi driver's bewildered expression.

He gazed at the same landscape, but to him, it remained an ordinary desert. 'I don't understand,' he muttered, shaking his head. 'What are you all looking at?'

'It's beautiful! Why are you not seeing it?' Adam's voice was filled with confusion.

Aunt Mary, Emma, and Adam exchanged amazed glances, realizing that what they were seeing might be a hidden wonder known only to those who truly believed in its existence. Emma leaned forward, eager to share their discovery with the taxi driver.

'You see, sir, it's not just a desert for us. We've been searching for this place, The Valley of Knowledge, and it's like a secret world within a world.' Emma said.

The taxi driver's confusion deepened, but he couldn't help but be intrigued by their passion and conviction. 'It's like something out of a legend,' he said, still shaking his head in disbelief–poor guy.

Adam nodded. His eyes were fixed on the pyramid-like structure in the distance. 'Exactly! It's as if this place exists for those who truly believe in its magic and its history. And we're here to unlock its secrets.'

As they approached the oasis, Aunt Mary leaned closer to the taxi driver. 'Thank you for your help. We couldn't have found this place without you. It's a discovery we'll cherish forever.' and she's got this warm smile that's practically a ray of sunshine. She's all classy and grateful.

The taxi driver, still bewildered but touched by their appreciation. 'Well, I may not understand it, but I'm glad I could be a part of your adventure.' But hey, he'll be sharing this tale with his fellow taxi drivers for years to come. The day he drove some folks to the invisible oasis in the desert. Crazy, right?

With a sense of gratitude and excitement, they exited the taxi and began their journey into The Valley of Knowledge.

'So, you two, we get it, right? Our bond with this valley is something special.' Aunt Mary said.

'Totally, Aunt Mary. This place is incredible, and I can't wait to see what's next.' Emma said.

Aunt Mary, Adam, and Emma turned to the taxi driver, who still looked puzzled.

'Well, we're gonna explore a bit more. Hang tight, and we'll come back when we're done with our research.' Aunt Mary said to the taxi driver.

'I guess I'll wait, but this is all a bit strange to me. Have a great time exploring this... hidden paradise, or whatever it is!' The taxi driver said as he saw the three of them vanish into thin air.

With a shared understanding and a sense of gratitude for their unique connection to the valley, Aunt Mary, Adam, and Emma stepped forward, ready to embark on the next chapter of their adventure, leaving the taxi driver still puzzled by the mystery.

They're determined to uncover the secrets of this hidden wonder. And why is it invisible to some? The others still didn't understand why the place was only visible to people who believed in its existence.

Emma's got her excitement out, and Adam's ready to decode some hieroglyphs.

So, with the backdrop of this mysterious oasis and the grand pyramid, they're ready to uncover the secrets of this unique place and, well, explore it like the true adventurers they are.

Chapter 4
Unveiling the Message

Adam, Emma, and Aunt Mary stood at the entrance of The Valley of Knowledge.

So, like, when they reached where they thought was the entrance to The Valley of Knowledge, it wasn't this grand, ancient gate or anything. It was more like a vibe, a symbol of the connection between the past and the present, a place where the quest for knowledge and the unraveling of secrets would continue. It was like the universe saying, 'Hey! This is the entrance.' It was like they were guided by the invisible hand of destiny.

Their hearts are filled with hope and wonder. The lush oasis before them seemed to beckon them forward, promising hidden secrets and ancient wisdom.

Their journey began with a thorough exploration of The Valley of Knowledge's extensive library, a genuine meadow of wisdom snuggled within the hidden oasis. This place was like a field of wisdom, hidden away in the middle of nowhere. Can you believe it? It's like, 'Hey, let's put all the knowledge in the world in this random desert oasis.'

'This place is incredible, Emma. It's like nothing I've ever seen.' Adam said.

'I know. I can't even believe I'm seeing this.' Emma replied.

Rows and rows of bookshelves, like an ancient book lover's dream, were stretching out before them. These wooden shelves were groaning under the weight of books so old they had wrinkles. It was like a library from the time of the pharaohs, preserved through the ages.

What struck them immediately was the remarkable organization of the books. The way these texts were organized was like something out of a librarian's wildest fantasies. It was like the books put *themselves* in perfect order. Each ancient text was precisely cataloged, creating a sense of order within the fountain of knowledge. Those old scrolls and manuscripts were lined up like well-behaved soldiers, and you could almost hear them saying, 'At your service, knowledge-hungry explorers!' The shelves seemed to hold the gathered wisdom of generations, waiting to be unearthed.

Adam was in his element, calm and collected as ever. He gave a nod, his eyes glued to those ancient bookshelves. 'It's mind-blowing, really. I mean, just look at how these texts are organized. It's like they were waiting for us, all neat and tidy. But,' he added, his voice steady, 'deciphering these hieroglyphs? Now that's the real adventure.'

Adam, with his sharp eye for deciphering puzzles, embarked on the laborious task of examining the hieroglyphs within these ancient texts. He focused on the intricate symbols, searching for any distinct patterns that might offer a glimpse into the script they had discovered. His efforts revealed a horde of symbols, numbering well into the hundreds. Realizing the complexity of the task, he understood that decoding the hieroglyphic typescripts would require the expertise of a seasoned historian or linguist.

'This is *much* more complex than I thought. Decoding the hieroglyph is gonna be a monumental task.' Adam said.

'You're right, Adam. We might need some expert help to tackle this.' Emma agreed.

What Adam indeed sought was a key, a script, or a guide that could seamlessly translate Egyptian hieroglyphs into a modern language. He knew that such a discovery would be a crucial step in unraveling the mysteries hidden within the mysterious script.

'I think what we need is a key—a way to translate these hieroglyphs into a modern language. That's the key to understanding this script.' Adam said.

'Yeah, that would really help us in translating the hieroglyph.' Emma replied.

Meanwhile, Emma, with her resourceful nature, embarked on a quest to uncover the history of The Valley of Knowledge itself. She believed that a deeper understanding of the valley's origins and the reasons behind its hidden existence might hold the key to their quest. Emma scoured the shelves not only for books but also for maps, guides, or any literature that would spotlight the valley's past.

She wasn't leaving any papyrus unturned, no dusty book unread. It was like watching a librarian on a mission to uncover the most mysterious gossip about ancient Egypt. She muttered to herself, 'There must be something in this library of ancient knowledge.'

'I'm gonna look for any information about the history of this place. Maybe that will give us some clues about why it exists and what secrets it holds.' Emma said. 'Or... maybe I'll find a user manual for this place?'

'Ha!' Adam gave a short laugh at Emma's mention of 'user manual.' 'Good idea, Emma. Let's split our efforts and cover all angles.'

'Right! That'll make our work faster and easier.'

Adam cracked up and said, 'Emma, if you find a cheat code to unlock the mysteries here, don't forget to share it with us.'

As they delved into the texts, they couldn't help but wonder about the ancient caretakers of this remarkable place. Who were they, and why had they chosen to preserve such a wealth of knowledge in this hidden oasis? With each page they turned, they hoped to uncover clues that would bring them closer to the truth, ultimately guiding them on their journey of discovery.

'I can't help but wonder who the ancient keepers of this place were. What motivated them to hide away this knowledge here?' Emma said.

'I'm wondering the same. Why was it even necessary to hide all these books?'

'It's a mystery. All this knowledge had to be kept out of the wrong hands.' Aunt Mary suggested

'That is logical.' Emma said. 'Maybe we should start leaving some notes ourselves,' Emma suggested jokingly. 'In case someone in the future is as baffled as we are.'

'Ha!' Adam gave a short laugh.

'Let's just keep searching.' Aunt Mary didn't want to waste any more time cracking jokes.

After a while, Emma's attention went towards the pyramid. 'Hey! We never checked the pyramid.'

'Right!' Aunt Mary said.

'Hmm. When I saw this place, the first thing I noticed was the pyramid, but later, when I saw the rows of bookshelves, my attention was diverted.' Adam said.

'Then? We must see what it contains.'

The three of them walked towards the pyramid.

'If the pyramid contains anything, then it must have an entrance...'

'We need to search for it.'

The three of them searched for the entrance. They searched every single side, but they had no luck finding an entrance.

'I guess that the pyramid has nothing to tell, then,' Adam said.

'I guess so,' Emma said.

'We must go back to whatever we were doing before.' Aunt Mary suggested. Saying this, all of them went back to their previous research.

Days turned into weeks as they immersed themselves in their research, pausing only to share their findings and speculate about the true nature of the script.

All three of them thought that the giant pyramid was solid and there was nothing inside, as they never saw any gateway to enter it. This was until–

'Finally. A map of The Valley of Knowledge,' Emma exhaled.

'Adam! Aunt Mary!' Emma called out.

'Hmm... What is it, Emma?' Adam asked.

'It's a map of The Valley of Knowledge. I want you to check whether it can be helpful to us in any way.' Emma replied.

'Well, a map is always helpful to navigate. Well, it is like... a user manual.'

'Ha! Then I *was* right.'

'Yeah! It might guide us to a place we haven't searched yet. Let me see,' Adam said as he took the map... or user manual from Emma.

Adam closely observed the map. It included places that they had searched. It also included the giant pyramid. It was the only place they hadn't explored. That was because they knew it had no visible entrance. But there was something odd on the map. The map showed that there was an entrance on each side of the pyramid. None of them had ever seen an entrance on any side of the pyramid. It was sealed.

'Emma, do you see this? This map says that there is an entrance on each side of the pyramid. Let's go and see. I don't think I saw an entrance anywhere.' Adam said with doubt.

They all went to each side of the pyramid and searched for hieroglyphs, seams, and inscriptions, but it seemed like there was no entrance. In fact, there was no clue either.

'Do you think we'll have to dig through the wall? I think that's the only way.' Emma said.

'Yeah. That's the only possible way, but how do we dig through the wall?' Adam said with expectation and confusion.

'You could have told me. I would have gotten a shovel.' Aunt Mary said.

'How are we supposed to know that we would need to *dig*?' Adam replied, and Aunt Mary went back to her research.

'I wish that there was an entrance,' Emma said.

'Yeah. Me too,' Adam agreed.

But then they heard a rumbling sound, and the ground started vibrating. Aunt Mary, who had been busy with her research, rushed to them when she felt the vibration. A part of the wall crumbled into the shape of an entrance, and all of them were shocked.

'What did you say, Emma? You're so... I don't have any words to explain.' Adam had been so excited for the first time that Emma was shocked.

If you didn't understand what just happened, when Emma wished for a door, the entrance revealed itself. I know that it's too good to be true.

Emma's revelation about their newfound power left them all in awe. It was like having their own personal genie grant them access to hidden treasures.

'I'm still wrapping my head around this. How is this even possible?' Adam confessed, trying to process the unexplainable events that had occurred throughout their journey.

Aunt Mary, always the logical one, chimed in, 'Well, whatever it is, we can't deny it's been working in our favor. We're now faced with an open door. Let's not keep this pyramid waiting.'

They decided to venture into the heart of the valley, where the ancient pyramid stood as a sentinel of the past.

The three explorers, Aunt Mary thinking of what had actually happened, entered the pyramid with a mixture of excitement and nervousness, unsure of what they might find within its ancient chambers.

Inside that giant, ancient pyramid, things got even crazier! They were greeted by a breathtaking sight. The walls were adorned with intricate hieroglyphs depicting stories of gods, pharaohs, and the mysteries of the afterlife. It was like they were in a time machine. Hieroglyphs were everywhere. But no, that's not the crazy part. What truly astonished them was the discovery that awaited on the pyramid's floor.

Laying there, right on the pyramid floor, was a parchment that could be the twin of the one they found in Professor Mitchell's room. I'm talking about the same texture, the same size, and even the same color. Also, the ink smelled exactly the same! The only visible difference was the script written on the parchment and the language in which it was written.

Adam, Emma, and Aunt Mary exchanged glances as they realized the significance of this discovery. It was clear that their journey had brought them closer to unraveling the mystery, but it had also raised countless questions. What was the connection between the two parchments? The three of them stared at each other, jaws dropping and all. You could see the bewildering expressions on their faces. I mean, who wouldn't be puzzled by two perfectly similar parchments showing up in two totally different places? Time-space mysteries right there!

'This is haunting me now. How is this possible? Is this some kind of trail that someone in our family might have left? Someone like our parents?' Adam said. His voice reflected that this situation was truly haunting her.

'You could be right. But if our parents left a trail, how could the parchment suddenly appear on Professor Mitchell's table? Wouldn't we have discovered the parchment long ago?' Emma replied. She, too, was stammering.

'I don't think we would have discovered it before. Since we were young, Professor Mitchell and Aunt Mary kept the room locked. Even if it wasn't locked, it was never wide open. But this leaves us with a question. Who opened the door on the day you discovered the parchment?' Adam explained.

'Aunt Mary, did you open the door on that day?' Emma asked.

'Oh, I would never do that. It was probably Professor Mitchell. He might have forgotten to close the door.'

Adam's eyes nearly popped out of his head, 'Wait, Professor Mitchell was there? And you forgot to tell us?'

Aunt Mary casually said, 'I guess it slipped my mind, sweetie.' She said it like it was nothing much of a deal. It's like inviting a guest and forgetting to tell the others who live at your house that a guest is coming.

'Okay, mystery solved, kind of.' Adam said, 'This must be a trail from our parents.' Adam picked up the parchment and slipped it into his pocket like it was the most normal thing in the world.

'Let's go. We still have to decode the hieroglyph.' Aunt Mary said, eager to know the mystery behind the hieroglyph.

'Yeah. Let's decode these hieroglyphs!'

With the newfound parchment in their possession, they knew that they had to continue their search for answers. The Valley of Knowledge held more secrets than they could have ever imagined, and they were determined to unveil them, one mystery at a time.

'Hey, Adam. You know what? Let's all wish for a Latin phonetic to Egyptian hieroglyph translation,' Emma said with wonder.

'You sure it will work?'

'Eh, why not give it a shot? It's worth trying. Isn't it?' Emma replied, confident that her plan would work.

Adam liked the idea. So they all closed their eyes and wished for the weirdest thing ever. They wished for a book containing a Latin phonetic to Egyptian hieroglyph translation. Sounds strange for a wish, right? Imagine that you are a genie, and someone wishes not for a million dollars or world peace but for a 'Latin phonetic to Egyptian hieroglyph translation.' Just your everyday genie stuff, right?

And guess what? After they wished, they waited for a while. Nothing happened, but then, boom! They heard a rattling sound inside the pyramid. Of course, they were thinking that some ancient curse was about to unleash mummies or something.

'What just happened?' Adam exclaimed when he heard the mysterious rattling sound. He was a bit terrified, too. I think it's understandable why.

'I don't know. But I'm sure that the sound came from inside the pyramid.' Emma wondered what the sound might be.

Adam seemed to realize something. 'Wait, I did notice the bookshelves in the pyramid move. The sound might be from there. I'll go and check. Come with me.' Adam took them in.

The two went to the pyramid. Adam showed Emma the bookshelves and told her to check what had happened.

They were checking out the bookshelves when Adam spotted something fishy.

'Emma, do you see that book sticking out? Everything is perfectly aligned, but not that book. That is what might have caused the rattling sound.'

'Yeah. I see that.' Emma noticed that there was a book sticking out.

They were like, 'Well, well, well, what do we have here?' and both went to check out the book. It was just what they had wanted. It was a book, but it looked newer than the rest of the books. Its cover page read-

LATIN - AEGYPTII

'This book must've been written by the Romans,' Adam said. 'The Egyptians declined before the rise of the Romans. So, there is no way that the Egyptians knew Latin. This can also be said as the book looks newer than the others.' Indeed, it was different from the rest. It was newer and had Roman vibes.

'So, does that mean the Romans knew about this place?'

'Probably yes. So now that we have the key to unlocking the mystery, why don't we make use of it?'

Adam and Emma spent hours deep into the night like a couple of hieroglyphic detectives. They were all fine with the simple ones, you know, the hands-like things, the eyes with no pupil, and the candy stick, but when it came to birds, they were scratching their heads like, 'Is this a W or an A?' And when I say birds, I mean these:

They look so identical, right?

'Why are there so many birds that look identical? A, and W. Which one is what?' Emma shouted.

'Calm down. I might have made a mistake while copying it down. I never thought that such minor details would be important. Let's roll with both birds being 'W' for now. That's the closest to both.'

This is what they had decoded–

IST TWWRDS RA.

'*Ist twawards ra?* What's that, some ancient Egyptian song lyrics?' Emma asked Adam.

Adam said with a smile. 'No, Emma. In Egyptian mythology, "Ra" refers to "the sun" or the "sun god".' This is all I can say.'

'So, ist twawards the sun?' Emma asked.

Adam put his thinking cap on and figured, 'Ist twawards the sun... that sounds like an English sentence to me!'

'Ist twawards the sun...' Emma thought for a while. 'Yeah! I know. East towards the sun. But well, what does that mean?'

'It may refer to something that always points towards the east. Mostly something Egyptian.' Adam replied. 'I think we'll need to know more about Egypt.'

Emma had a bright idea. 'Hey, why don't we ask someone in Cairo about this? They've got to know their own history, right?

'Clever! Aunt Mary, we'll go back to Cairo.' Adam said, ready to decode the mystery behind the sentence, East towards the sun.

'Huh? Oh! Sure.' Aunt Mary replied.

They exited the beautiful valley and walked towards the taxi. The taxi driver was waiting for them.

As they came into sight, the taxi driver spoke up, 'So, what did you do there for five weeks? You'll have to pay a lot.'

Emma, with her enthusiasm, shrugged off the time and replied, 'Five weeks? It felt like a breeze!'

'How did you even survive for five weeks?' Adam was curious, as there was no way that the taxi driver could have survived for such a long time.

'I did starve, but it's a good thing I had some snacks in my bag. By the way, a helpful passerby provided me with enough supplies.'

'Wow!' Adam exclaimed.

What the taxi driver said was indeed not true. The taxi driver had a secret. Let me tell you the secret.

So, the taxi driver had slipped a microphone into Adam's unzipped bag. And well, it's Adam's bag, so he did not notice. As they entered The Valley of Knowledge, so did the microphone in Adam's bag.

The taxi driver waited there for a while or so, and... he went back to Cairo for his regular task of taxi trips. So... he was getting his regular wage, and he also added on to Aunt Mary's waiting time fare. So clever, right? But you must be asking, How did the taxi driver know when they would come out, right? That's where the microphone comes in.

He had been listening to their conversations all along. And by all conversations, I really do mean *all*. Then, when the taxi driver got to know that they were almost done with their work, well, you know what happened. See? And the taxi driver was pretending as if he didn't know anything. How untrustworthy he was!

'We'll go back to Cairo.' Aunt Mary told the taxi driver as she started to become impatient. And then, the taxi driver slipped the microphone out of Adam's unzipped bag so that they wouldn't find it later on. Why is Adam so careless?

The taxi driver drove back to Cairo. It was, again, a long journey. The three of them kept on thinking about how they spent five weeks like it was nothing.

As they left The Valley of Knowledge behind and embarked on their journey back to Cairo, they couldn't help but reflect on the incredible discoveries they had made. The taxi ride gave them a chance to engage in some informal conversation about their experiences.

Aunt Mary, with a chuckle, remarked, 'Who would've thought that wishing for an entrance could actually make one appear? It's like something out of a fairy tale.'

Adam nodded in agreement, a smile playing on his lips. 'Yeah, it's unbelievable how our thoughts or words can make stuff happen. What an unexpected twist in our adventure! This adventure's been one wild ride!'

After they reached Cario, the taxi driver seemed really happy. He was calculating the total fare like a math whiz. His excitement was much like Emma's

'Okay.' The taxi driver started. 'So, Cairo to Alexandria will be 300 EGP. Another 300 for returning. The waiting time was 20 EGP per hour the day you booked the taxi, and the total waiting time was 836 hours, which gives us 16720 EGP. Totally, we get 17320 EGP.' The taxi driver said happily. Now you know why he was so happy.

'Ok. You gave us the total fare, I believe.' Aunt Mary asked.

'Yeah!'

'And what is EGP?'

'Oh! I forgot. You're from America, right? Well, EGP is Egyptian Pounds, and 17320 Egyptian Pounds would be about 2712 USD.'

Oh yes, to those people who are wondering why 17320 EGP converts to $2712, well, the value of one dollar rises and falls every month like a rollercoaster. Wait, not every month, but every minute. Around the year 2003, one EGP was equal to $0.16.

Aunt Mary paid the fare. She got a change of 27 EGP, 80 piastres.

'You just dropped twenty-seven grand, just on a taxi?' Adam was surprised when he saw Aunt Mary pay twenty-seven grand with ease.

'Yeah, but who cares?' Aunt Mary shrugged it off like she was a billionaire or something. 'It's all for the sake of our research, folks!'

The taxi driver, overhearing their conversation, chimed in, 'You folks must be some kind of explorer wizards or something.'

Adam, with a grin, replied, 'You could say that. We're on a mission to decode ancient mysteries. And guess what? Sometimes, all it takes is a wish to open doors, literally!'

The taxi driver looked at them like they were the protagonists of some wild adventure movie. 'Wow! You folks have a way crazier life than I do. I'm just a good old taxi driver.'

Chapter 5
Mystery behind the Message

Before asking anyone about what the message might mean, they tried to figure it out by themselves.

Adam, always the calm and collected one, said, 'Guys, I think we should put on our thinking caps and try to decipher this thing ourselves before we go bothering others.'

Emma, with a thoughtful expression, added, 'The message was 'East towards the sun,' right?'

Adam nodded. 'Yeah, that's it.'

'But

'But *what* does that even mean in the context of our quest? It must be a clue to something significant. It can't be as simple as 'head east until you see the sunrise' or something, right?'

They all scratched their heads, going through a mental Rolodex of all the Egyptian culture, history, and architecture they had ever heard of (which, honestly, wasn't much). But nothing seemed to click.

'We seem to have only one option,' Adam said.

'Yeah. I know. The only option is to ask someone who thoroughly knows about Egypt. Let's not go wandering off into the desert with no clue. We need some local insight or expertise.' Emma replied.

'Aunt Mary, we are back to plan A. We'll have to find a true Egyptian.' Adam said.

They went all across Cairo, asking people whether they had any idea of what East towards the sun could mean. No one had any idea. They were all either tourists or Egyptian citizens who came from other countries.

Aunt Mary, with her undiminished patience, would politely approach people and inquire, 'Excuse me, but do you have any idea about what 'East towards the sun' might mean?'

The responses varied from absolute ignorance to confusion, with locals and tourists scratching their heads, thinking about what it might mean. Some would reply, 'No, I have no idea.' while others would admit, 'I'm just a tourist.'

They had asked so many people that they were almost about to quit until Aunt Mary found a person.

'Are you an Egyptian?' Aunt Mary asked.

'*Ana la aerif allughat al iinjilizia.*' The person said.

As Adam thought about what the person was saying, he couldn't help but share his insights with Aunt Mary and Emma.

'What was that?' Emma was confused.

'I think he's speaking Arabic,' Adam remarked, his voice tinged with frustration. 'This is the challenge of having to communicate with a true Egyptian. We need a translator, someone who can bridge the gap between him and us.'

Aunt Mary, always resourceful and quick to take action, nodded in agreement. 'I'll do my best to find a translator,' she said, determination in her eyes. She left in search of someone who could assist them in their communication.

Adam and Emma ensured that the person Aunt Mary found wouldn't slip away. They understood that the presence of a skilled translator would be a crucial step.

After a few minutes, Aunt Mary returned with a person. He looked resourceful.

'This is Amir Khalid. He is a visitor from Saudi Arabia. He accepted my request to be a translator for a few minutes.'

'Can you ask this person for his name?' Adam asked Amir.

'*Ma asmuk.*' Amir asked the person.

'*Ana Tarek Ibrahim,*' The person replied.

'He says that his name is Tarek Ibrahim.'

'Ok. Ask him whether he's an Egyptian by birth.'

'*Tarek, hal 'ant misriun bialwiladati?*'

'*Naem.*'

'He *is* Egyptian by birth,' Amir said.

'Ask him whether he knows about Egyptian culture and Architecture.'

'*Hal taruf an althaqafatih walmrath almisryat*'

'*La, lakiniy 'aerif shkhsan qad yafeal dhalika. wayuetaqid 'ana rahbaan yaeish fi maebad alkarinki. lam yatamakan siwaa shakhs wahid min aleuthur ealayhi. kan aismuh mitshil wilsun. 'Iidha kunt qadran ealaa aleuthur ealaa hadha alraahibi, faqad yakun qadran ealaa musaeadatik.*'

'Uh... What did he say?' Emma asked Amir.

'Hmm... I don't think I can remember everything he said. He said he doesn't know about Egyptian culture and architecture, but a monk in Karnak Temple might. I think he said that only one person has ever met him. I wasn't able to catch his name properly. It was Mitsel Wilson or something.'

The mention of Mitsel Wilson had them all exchanging puzzled glances, their eyebrows performing a complicated interpretive dance. 'Wait a minute,' they collectively wondered. Could Mitsel

Wilson be some long-lost relative of Professor Mitchell Wilson? Or maybe it's Professor Mitchell Wilson himself.

'Oh! I remember this belief. It was about the monk Anthony the Great. He was believed to have been a Roman monk who escaped the fall of Rome by traveling to Egypt. Since then, he had been hiding in the Karnak temple.' Amir added on.

'So, doesn't that mean he'll be speaking Latin?' Adam asked.

'Mostly yes.'

'Dad taught me Latin, but...'

'But you forgot. Right?' Emma interrupted

'Uh... Yeah'

'I know Latin.' Aunt Mary said.

Emma's eyes widened, like she'd just discovered a hidden treasure. 'Hold up, Aunt Mary, you speak Latin? Are you secretly a time-traveling scholar or something? I mean, pilot, Latin, what's next? Are you also fluent in Martian?' Her tone was filled with mock suspicion, adding a hilarious twist to the conversation.

Aunt Mary just chuckled mysteriously. 'Well, dear, a lady has to have her secrets. And who knows, maybe I'm also an expert in talking to dolphins or decoding ancient alien messages,' she teased Adam and Emma, who couldn't help but burst into laughter.

'Okay, then. We have all the information that we need.' Adam said.

'You can tell Tarek to go. Give him this 20 EGP,' Aunt Mary told Amir.

'*Shukran Tarek. Tastatie alrahil. Khudh hadhih al eishrin jnyhan*,' Amir said to Tarek and gave him the 20 EGP. Tarek left.

'You can also leave. You have been of great help.' Aunt Mary said. She gave him $5, and Amir left.

'We'll need to go to the Karnak temple,' Adam said to Aunt Mary as Amir and Tarek left.

'I know. I'll have to find a taxi.' Aunt Mary said and then went to find a taxi. Adam and Emma continued their conversation.

'This time, we're not spending five weeks,' Adam said. Last time at the Valley of Knowledge, they spent five whole weeks just decoding the hieroglyph.

Emma thought about what Adam said about spending five weeks. 'Wait. When did we leave?' Emma asked.

'I guess around May 30th,' Adam said. I have no idea how he remembers the date, so don't ask.

Emma gasped dramatically. 'Did we just lose track of time? I mean, our school starts in August, and we can't just waltz in with our 'we went on an ancient Egyptian adventure' excuse.' Emma said.

'Yeah, let's add 'surviving school' to our list of grand adventures. It's gonna be wild!' Adam said as they both shared an amused grin.

Adam and Emma waited until Aunt Mary got a taxi. They discussed the Karnak temple and whether Professor Mitchel had really been there or not.

'Do you think that when Amir said Mitsel Wilson, he was talking about Professor Mitchell Wilson?' Emma asked.

'I know, right? When he said Mitsel Wilson, all I could think of was uncle's name.'

'By the way, he said that he *didn't* catch the name right. It's evident that he had gotten the name wrong.'

Suddenly, Aunt Mary chimed in. 'I found a taxi to Karnak temple.'

'Let's go to the Karnak temple, then,' Adam said, concluding the talk about Professor Mitchell.

Aunt Mary took them to the taxi. They boarded the taxi.

The taxi took them to the Karnak temple.

As they hopped into the taxi, Emma couldn't contain her excitement. 'Off to Karnak, we go! Buckle up, folks. It's time for another round of ancient mysteries and monks!'

Adam chimed in, 'Seriously, though, what if we find some ancient scrolls, and they magically reveal all the secrets of the universe? Or at least, the secret to acing all our exams.'

Aunt Mary, who was observing the Cairo traffic like she was driving, laughed.

And off they went, weaving through Cairo's bustling streets, fueled by excitement and the promise of more thrilling discoveries.

They reached the Karnak temple.

'Please wait here until we come back.' Aunt Mary told the taxi driver.

The Karnak temple was not as appealing as The Valley of Knowledge, as it had significantly less greenery.

After all, what they came for was the monk Anthony the Great. So, greenery didn't matter.

They entered the Karnak temple. There were detailed carvings and hieroglyphs on each wall.

'Look at these carvings and hieroglyphs. They're incredibly detailed. Seriously, these Egyptians were the original overachievers when it came to decorating their place.' Adam said.

'We've got the key to decoding them.' Emma said. '... So, we could decode them, right?'

'I'm not sure we have time to decipher every single one. After all, that's not what we are here for.'

'Right! Let's focus on what we are here for.'

'You're right. We can always come back later for a closer look. Let's focus on finding that monk for now.'

Off they went, exploring the temple with a mission–not to become Egyptology experts but to unlock the secrets that the place held.

'This temple is massive. It feels like it goes on forever.' Emma said

It does. I wonder how deep it goes. We should keep moving. Maybe we'll find the monk further inside.' Adam said

They proceed, leaving the intricate hieroglyphs for another time as they venture deeper into the seemingly endless temple.

Emma sighed dramatically, 'This temple is like a maze, seriously. I half-expect to find a Minotaur guarding some treasure at this point.'

Adam laughed, 'Or maybe a mummy that just wants a good conversation. Who knows?'

'Well, I hope it's not too talkative. We're here to find answers, not listen to ancient ghost stories!'

Despite the jokes, they kept moving deeper and deeper into the temple, wondering if they were going in circles or getting closer to their mysterious monk. It was like a never-ending adventure.

They walked for hours until they heard a voice.

Quid tu hic agis?

They were terrified. They couldn't see the person who was talking.

'Who are you? Show yourself!' Adam said.

Quis es? Estisne Aegyptii?

'Huh?' Emma could not understand a single word.

'It's Latin. He's asking whether we are Egyptians or not. Let me try.' Aunt Mary said

'No, non sumus Aegyptii.' She said to the voice.

Et unde venistis?

'Ex America sumus. Et cur nos rogasti ubi sumus?' Aunt Mary replied.

Emma was perplexed about what they were saying. Adam could understand a little bit.

Ego sum Antonius. Monachus Romanus. Populus Aegyptius me existimat, sed Aegyptiorum ex quo Roma fugi.

'Uh, what did the voice say?' Emma asked Aunt Mary.

'He is Anthony, the monk, and he has been scared of Egyptians since the time he escaped Rome. He thinks that we are here to harm him.'

'Non sumus hic nocere tibi. Hic sumus, quia auxilio tuo indigemus.' Aunt Mary said.

Quid a me tibi opus est auxilio?

'What did he ask?' Emma asked Aunt Mary.

'He wants to know about the help we need from him.'

'Do you know English?' Emma asked Anthony.

I know every language that uses the Latin phonetics. Anthony replied.

Emma rolled her eyes and asked, 'Why did we end up talking to you in Latin when you know English? And seriously, Aunt Mary, you've been speaking Latin for no reason!'

Anthony, with a cryptic smile, responded, *Because, my dear, sometimes the journey is more important than the destination.*

'That doesn't matter now,' Adam said. 'Anthony the Great, we have decoded an Egyptian hieroglyph to reveal the message, East towards the sun. Do you have any idea what it may mean?'

An Egyptian Hieroglyph? Sounds interesting. Oriente ad solem. It can refer to Egyptian architecture that always points towards the sun, which symbolizes 'order.' There are many such architectures that exist, but they may point in any other direction, such as the west or chaos, where the sun sets. But there is one structure–the Sphinx.

'But there are many sphinxes all over the world. Which one do you think it refers to?'

The Great Sphinx of Giza.

'Thanks for your help,' Aunt Mary said.

Gratias.

They started their walk out of the temple. They walked for a few hours. As they walked out of the temple, they saw the taxi driver waiting for them.

They boarded the taxi. This taxi driver didn't ask them what they did at the temple for such a long time, unlike the previous taxi driver. The taxi driver, not as chatty as the last one, kept his curiosity to himself. He probably thought, 'Well, they've been gone for hours, not weeks. They must've just had a super extended lunch break or something.'

Adam, Emma, and Aunt Mary didn't mind the time either. They were too focused on the cryptic task ahead. 'We'll go to the Great Sphinx of Giza,' Aunt Mary said.

The taxi driver drove them to the Great Sphinx of Giza, the oldest known monumental sculpture in Egypt.

Adam and Emma were in a bit of a pickle. The Sphinx was a pretty massive hunk of stone with a lion's body and a pharaoh's head, and they had zero ideas about where to start their search.

'Where do you think we have to search?' Adam asked with doubt.

'Well, nothing was mentioned in the message about where to search in the Sphinx, so we might have to search all over the Sphinx for any clues,' Emma said.

'We might as well have to go back to The Valley of Knowledge to search for any clues on where to start searching for any mystery.'

Emma, in her usual bright thinking, said, 'You know what, Adam? That parchment we snagged from the pyramid at The Valley of Knowledge. We never really took a crack at deciphering it. Maybe, just maybe, it's got some tips on where to begin our treasure hunt!'

'What Parchment?'

'Oh, my God! Why are you so forgetful? You don't remember the identical parchment that we found inside the pyramid at The Valley of Knowledge?'

Adam slapped his forehead, realizing he'd been forgetful. 'Oh, right, that old parchment! I've got it right here.' He reached into his pocket and pulled it out.

'Yeah, that one. We never tried decoding that. It might contain clues to where we need to search.'

'Hmm... This looks like a mix of Greek and some other language. We might try asking someone around who knows Greek.'

'Did anyone say Greek?' Aunt Mary interrupted.

'Yeah. I did. Translating this script into Greek might tell us where to start our search.'

'I am sorry that I did not tell this before, but I know Greek. Well, sort of.' Aunt Mary said. Her voice reflected her guilty feelings.

'Wow. Can you just tell us what you are hiding from us?' Emma was fed up with her aunt hiding things from them.

'I'll tell when required,' Aunt Mary said with a short smile.

'Now, can you tell us what this means?' Adam said, pointing towards the text on the parchment, which looked like this:

Λγνδ ἀς ιτ ζατ ζρ ις αυ μαζ βλω ζ παως
αωφ ιτ ζατ λαδς τυ ζ μυστρυ αωφ ζ ἀλ
αωφ ρcρδς ωρ αλ σντιαλ νωλδγ αωφ
αλ¢μυ αστρνμυ μαζματιcς μαηιc ανδ
μδιcιν ις στρδ.

Aunt Mary observed the text for a while.

'Uh, this is not pure Greek. It is just a Greek transliteration. It must be a transliteration from a Latin-based language to Greek.' Aunt Mary looked confused.

'I guess you should transliterate it back to Latin phonetics,' Adam suggested.

'I'll try.' She took Adam's notebook and pen and started transliterating.

After around ten minutes, Aunt Mary completed the transliteration. This is what she wrote:

Lgnd has it zat zr is ay maz blw z paws awf it zat lads tu z mystry awf z hal awf rcrds wr al sntial nwldg awf alcmy astrnmy mazmatics majic and mdicin is strd.

The three of them examined the parchment, but all they saw was what appeared to be a jumble of letters as if someone's cat had just run across a typewriter.

Emma voiced her frustration, 'What is this? It looks like some gibberish.'

'Yeah. It does look like some random letters.' Adam said.

Aunt Mary was quick to remind them, 'I know, but they are supposed to have some meaning.'

Adam caught onto the idea, saying, 'Yeah, it's probably coded in some way.'

'So, you mean that we need to decode it?' Emma asked.

'Yeah.'

Adam looked at the text carefully. He knew that it held some hidden secret that they did not know. He knew that it had some sort of clue.

'I think I found out how it is coded,' Adam said.

'You did?' Emma asked. Curious to know what the text means.

'Yeah. I found out that it's not gibberish. It's just that there are some missing vowels.' Adam explained.

'If there are missing vowels, How do we know where to put what vowel?' Emma asked.

'It's similar to the previous script, lst twwrds ra. We read it, and we replace it with the closest word that we get.' Adam replied.

'So, "Lgnd has it zat" should be 'Legend has it that,' right?'

'Yeah. We'll have to do it for the whole thing. Also, did you notice that the 'th' is replaced with 'z'?'

'Yeah. "that" is written as "zat,"' Emma agreed. 'So, if we do it for the complete script, it would be, Legend has it that there is a maze below the paws of it that...'

'Leads...'

'...that leads to the mystery of the hall of records, where all... sntial nwldg?'

Adam and Emma thought for a while. Finally, Adam spoke up. 'S – N – tial Naw - Ledj. It would be 'essential knowledge."

'So, where all essential knowledge of alchemy, astronomy, mathematics, magic, and medicine is... stored.'

Legend has it that there is a maze below the paws of it that leads to the mystery of the hall of records, where all essential knowledge of alchemy, astronomy, mathematics, magic, and medicine is stored. Adam thought about it for a while. 'This is it. We have to search below the paws of the Sphinx for a maze. But how do we do it without anyone noticing?'

'We'll need to do it under the cover of night. And as for the taxi driver, we should let him go, or he might raise the alarm.' Aunt Mary suggested.

Chapter 6
Deep Underground

Aunt Mary went to tell the taxi driver to go.

'The fare would be 250 EGP. Which will be 40 USD.' The taxi driver said. Aunt Mary paid $40, and the taxi driver drove away.

The moon hung low in the night sky, casting an ethereal glow over the Great Sphinx of Giza. Adam, Emma, and Aunt Mary stood near the colossal monument. Their breath was clearly visible in the chilly desert air.

A sense of anticipation and uncertainty hung in the air as they absorbed the parchment's message. 'Legend had it that beneath the paws of the Sphinx lay a maze, a gateway to the Hall of Records, where the ancient knowledge of alchemy, astronomy, mathematics, magic, and medicine was said to be stored.' It was a quest that had drawn them deeper into the heart of Egypt's mysteries.

With their plan set, they headed toward the Sphinx's massive stone body. Their footsteps were muffled by the desert sand. However, as they approached, they noticed an unexpected obstacle–a deep boundary encircling the Sphinx, preventing anyone from getting too close to its paws.

'What should we do?' Emma asked.

'This boundary is stopping us from reaching the paws of the Sphinx. We can't just climb down. It is really steep.' Adam mentioned.

They huddled together, brainstorming ideas in hushed voices. The boundary was extremely deep, and they needed a way to reach the maze hidden beneath the paws.

'I have an idea,' Aunt Mary whispered. 'We can use a rope ladder to climb down from the boundary.

'I was thinking the same, but where do we get such a long rope ladder?' Emma asked.

'We could tie a few rope ladders to make one,' Adam suggested.

'What if the knots untie? Our lives will be in danger.' Emma said.

'I know it's a risky plan, but it seems to be our best option.' Aunt Mary said. Hoping that their plan would work.

'What about the guards? We will also need to distract the guards who are patrolling the area to ensure that our activities go unnoticed.' Emma added on.

'Don't worry about them. I have an idea.' Aunt Mary said with confidence.

'What is it?' Emma asked, curious about what her aunt had planned.

'We can create a distraction so that the guards don't look at us when we climb down.'

'That would work, but how do we create the distractions?' Adam asked.

'I'll tell you later.'

As the moon inched its way up the night sky, they huddled together, ready for action. Aunt Mary gave a final briefing, making sure everyone was on the same page.

'Alright, it's almost time, folks.' Aunt Mary started. 'When that moon gets to its peak, we'll roll out our master plan. Remember, our goal is to distract those guards away from our precious target, The Sphinx.'

Emma, eager and determined, chimed in, 'I'm all set, Aunt Mary. So, what's the grand plan?'

Aunt Mary grinned like the mastermind she was, 'We'll put on a show of distractions. I've got a collection of little noisemakers. Pebbles and tin cans.

We'll create sudden disturbances at different spots around the Sphinx's pad. Those guards won't be able to resist their curiosity.'

Adam, the strategy expert who wins all chess matches, joined the conversation, 'Sounds like a cunning plan. And while one of us creates the disturbances, the others will tiptoe in the shadows, sticking close to the edge of the enclosure.'

Aunt Mary nodded approvingly, 'Absolutely. We'll mimic the guards' routines with slow and steady movements to avoid any raised eyebrows. Let's make them think it's just another night on the job.'

'And what about misdirection?' Emma asked

Emma wasn't done with her curiosity, though, 'And what about the art of misdirection?' She asked.

'We can scatter some bait items on the opposite side of the enclosure, implying a sneaky intruder. That should trick the guards into going further away from where we don't want them to be.'

Adam applauded, 'Very clever! Plus, we'll engage in hushed conversations, whispering about potential intruders to sell the whole drama. It'll be like an Oscar-worthy performance.'

'Exactly. By combining these elements, we'll divert the guards' attention and lure them to the Sphinx's enclosure. That will give us the opportunity to access the maze below the paws unnoticed. Once we're there, we'll get ready with the rope ladder.'

'Sounds like a solid plan. But first, we have to wait for that moon to do its part.' Adam said.

The moon rose higher, and it was time to execute their plan.

While one of them created the distractions, the others moved discreetly in the shadows. Aunt Mary and the siblings kept close to the boundary, ready to take cover if necessary.

As the guards began investigating the noises, Aunt Mary, the conductor of this grand orchestra of rocks and tin cans, ensured that their movements were as smooth as butter. They mimicked the guards' patrol routine, slow and steady, like it was just another routine night at the site.

They strategically placed some items that hinted at a possible intruder on the opposite side of the enclosure. This drew the guards further away from their intended location.

Aunt Mary and the siblings also engaged in hushed conversations, pretending to discuss a potential trespasser in the area. This, as planned, further fueled the guards' curiosity.

Aunt Mary and the siblings effectively diverted the guards' attention and lured them to a remote corner of the Sphinx's enclosure, giving themselves the opportunity to execute their primary intention of accessing the maze below the paws unnoticed. They stealthily approached the boundary with the rope ladder.

They climbed down into the deep elliptical pit. The air grew colder and denser as they went deeper into the ground.

'Great! We're down.' Adam whispered

'Yeah! Good that everything worked just as we planned.' Aunt Mary said.

'I see the entrance!' Emma whispered.

'Where is it?' Adam asked quietly.

'Over there.' Emma pointed to the right side of the right paw. The others saw the entrance, too.

'Isn't that too tiny?' Adam asked.

'Let's just go and see,' Emma said in a soft voice.

The three of them walked towards the entrance. It looked tiny from far away, but when they came closer, it seemed pretty big.

'This is the entrance. We must make sure that we don't get stuck in the maze forever.' Emma noted.

Keeping what Emma said in mind, they entered what looked like a very long corridor. They walked on for miles. They may also encounter a dead end if the legend is false.

Emma's resourcefulness and ability to navigate through the complex passages proved invaluable as they descended further into the depths.

Along the way, they stumbled upon other identical parchments, each filled with different scripts. Adam collected them, knowing they held untold secrets that could be useful later on.

After what felt like an eternity of winding passages and twists and turns, they stumbled upon a gate with a clearly noticeable inscription that read, 'Labyrinth of Records.' The name alone sent shivers down their spines. This was it. The maze that led to the Hall of Records.

'Alright, everyone, follow my lead. I'm good at navigating through mazes, and I've got a feeling we're close.' Emma said in a bossy tone.

'We're putting our trust in your instincts, Emma. Lead the way, oh great maze conqueror!' Adam chimed in, his tone a mix of humor and genuine encouragement.

'Let's do this. Even if we encounter dead ends or false paths, we won't give up.' Aunt Mary said.

As Emma was the one with the remarkable ability to navigate through, the others followed Emma's lead. Her keen instincts guided them through the complex maze. They encountered dead ends and false paths, but Emma's unwavering determination ensured they pressed on.

Now, do you think they'll navigate this labyrinth with ease, or are they about to dive into a complicated puzzle? Will their determination and Emma's instincts lead them to the Hall of Records, or will they find themselves in a never-ending maze of bewildering twists and turns? Hang on tight to find answers to all these questions.

After hours of navigating through the labyrinth, they emerged into a resonant chamber, which was dimly lit by only a few torches.

Before them stood another gate; this one had a sign bearing the words, 'The Hall of Records.'

'Look, we've made it! This chamber is impressive.' Emma said. She was proud that her instincts were strong enough to guide them through the complicated maze.

'What's in here? Is this where we find the ancient knowledge?' Aunt Mary asked.

'This is it—the result of our journey. 'The Hall of Records.' It is where ancient knowledge is said to be stored. We've come a long way.' Adam said, eager to enter. 'Let's not waste any time. Let's see what secrets this place holds.'

They exchanged meaningful glances, the weight of their discovery hanging heavily in the air. With expectancy coursing through their veins, they pushed open the gate and stepped into the Hall of Records, ready to unlock the secrets of the ages.

Inside the Hall of Records, the sight before them was magnificent. Towering shelves filled with ancient scrolls and manuscripts reached toward the ceiling, creating an aura of knowledge that resonated throughout the chamber.

'It's true! The legend is true!' Emma gasped. Her eyes were wide with wonder.

Adam nodded in agreement, a smile of awe on his face.

'Uh Huh. It's beautiful. Just imagine the centuries of knowledge stored in this place. God knows why the Egyptians were hiding in such a beautiful place.'

Aunt Mary, always practical and cautious, 'Yeah. It's beautiful and all. But what are we gonna find here? Another parchment or something?'

Adam replied. 'Let's see.'

They went deeper into the hall, their footsteps echoing in the spacious chamber, and they began to discover a wealth of knowledge. But then, a scent wafted into their nostrils, and it was no pleasant aroma.

'Woah! What's that smell?' Emma said with disgust.

'Smells like rotten eggs to me,' Adam said.

'Yeah! It smells like rotten eggs,' Aunt Mary agreed.

'Why in the world are rotten eggs hanging out in this knowledge-filled place?' Emma pondered, still trying to avoid inhaling deeply.

'Maybe someone thought this was the ancient Egyptian version of a fridge and left an egg in here, and, well, you know what happens next...' Adam joked, flashing a playful grin.

And guess what happens next? All of a sudden, a voice spoke up, startling all of them–

Gypsum is a naturally occurring mineral composed of calcium sulfate dihydrate. It is a soft and translucent mineral that is commonly found in sedimentary rock formations.

Hydrogen sulfide is a gas that is often responsible for the characteristic rotten egg smell. In environments where gypsum is present and oxygen is limited, sulfate-reducing bacteria can thrive. These microorganisms can use sulfate ions found in gypsum as electron acceptors in their metabolic processes. Sulfate-reducing bacteria reduce sulfate ions to produce hydrogen sulfide gas as a metabolic byproduct. This gas is responsible for the rotten egg smell due to its characteristic odor. The voice dropped a mineralogy lecture like a bomb.

'Wait, who's our surprise lecturer? Did Albert Einstein just join the quest?' Emma raised her eyebrows.

'I do see some gypsum over there,' Aunt Mary casually pointed out.

'Ah... So that's what's causing the rotten egg stench,' Adam said.

'Gypsum? Where's that, and by the way, what's gypsum anyway?' Emma inquired with a classic 'I'm lost' expression.

'Didn't the surprise lecturer just drop some knowledge about gypsum?' Adam asked.

'Yeah, but do you think I paid attention?'

'Hmm... That explains it.'

'I see something.' Adam interrupted.

'What?' Emma asked

'A button.'

It was at this moment that Emma realized she was the culprit behind the unexpected lecture on minerals. 'Uh... I think I know who our surprise lecturer is.'

'You do?'

'I think so. I was walking, and I must've accidentally mashed that button, which triggered our geography lecture.'

'You mean to say it was a speaker? Impossible!' Adam protested.

'Can't we just pretend this never happened?' Aunt Mary seemed to be eager to carry on with their adventure while ignoring the scientific interruption.

'Sure! Let's just say that Egypt was in the future...' And then Adam was spellbound by something. 'What's that? The periodic table?!' Adam exclaimed as he saw a periodic table.

The periodic table was in the form of a shelf, and every compartment had the actual element. Even gases were there. They were all stored in glass bottles.

'Uh... What is this 'periodic table' you are talking about?' Emma asked, confused about what the periodic table is. I mean, you can't blame her. She's just nine years old.

Aunt Mary stepped in to explain, 'It's like a special list of all the tiny building blocks that make up everything around us, even the air we breathe.'

'Then... how is it useful?'

'You see, scientists have named these tiny building blocks as 'elements,' and the periodic table helps us organize them.'

'Nice. I am learning something new!' Emma said.

'Okay. Now, coming back to our mission, I think every single element is there.' Adam said.

'No, zinc is missing.' Aunt Mary corrected as she observed the periodic table.

When she said so, Adam was probably thinking, 'I thought Emma was the one with keen eyes.' But then, Emma had only a brief understanding of the periodic table. Adam spoke up. 'Right. Zinc is missing. And... why do you think it is missing?'

'Could be a clue.' Aunt Mary suggested.

They strolled further into the hall and found detailed documents about alchemy and accurate details about the universe.

'Check this out, guys! We strolled further into the hall, and, whoa, there's all this cool stuff.' Adam said as he noticed the documents.

'Really? What kind of cool stuff are we talking about here?' Aunt Mary was curious to know what he had found.

'Well, there are detailed documents about alchemy, like the real deal. And there's info about the universe that's *totally* on point.' Adam said.

'Plus, some mechanical gizmos that seem *way* too complex to be from the Ancient Egyptians,' Emma added.

However, as they continued their exploration, a faint but distinct smell reached their noses. No, not rotten eggs. It was an aroma suggestive of iron.

Emma furrowed her brow, her senses tingling. 'Do you smell that, Adam?'

'Yeah. But it smells familiar.' Adam said.

'Yeah. It's totally familiar. It's like the ink on the parchment we found.'

Adam nodded in agreement, his keen senses now on high alert. 'You're right, Emma. It's definitely the same smell.'

With every step they took, the scent grew stronger, leading them to a hidden corner of the chamber. There was a massive pile of parchments, just like the ones they found the clues in. There, they spotted a shawl with intricate details. It looked too new to be from Ancient Egypt... or even Rome.

Aunt Mary recognized it immediately, her voice catching with emotion. 'That's... that's the shawl your mother used to wear before she went out that day and disappeared without a trace.' She picked up the shawl and stuffed it in Adam's bag.

'This doesn't seem right,' Adam said.

'Our parents must have visited this place,' Emma suggested as a possible explanation.

'Yeah. That's the only logical explanation.' Aunt Mary said.

A heavy silence hung in the air, filled with unspoken questions and emotions. The shawl represented a tangible connection to the past, to the mystery surrounding their parents' disappearance, and to the secrets hidden within the Hall of Records.

As they stood in that moment, they knew they had stumbled upon something extraordinary–a revelation that was deeply personal. Their quest had taken an unexpected turn, and they were determined to uncover the truth that lay hidden within the ancient hall.

'The shawl, parchment, and the ink somehow seem to be connected,' Adam suggested.

Right! We already guessed that the parchments were from our parents, but what about the ink? Why iron?' Emma said, her voice filled with curiosity.

'I have no idea how the shawl is here,' Adam said. 'And as for the ink, it could be the ink that the Egyptians used... But why were our parents using it?'

'I think it is iron gall ink. Your uncle used to use it for everything, just to give it a vintage feel. It could be the same ink.' Aunt Mary said.

'What about these parchments? All of them are empty.' Emma said as she checked every single parchment.

'Check all of them.'

Emma checked every single parchment. After a hundred parchments or so, she found a parchment with something written on it.

Chapter 7
Path Out Wisdom

Emma glanced at what was written on the paper.

'English? This will be easy.' Emma said with confidence, which did not remain after she read what was written.

This is what was written:

When yon table's loom hath woven
grace,
A tapestry in heavenly space,
A cosmic waltz in high expanse,
To secrets veiled and wisdom's chance.

At morrow's end, with sun's last ray,
The stars, aligned, shall gently sway,
Above the empire zinc's embrace,
Reveals a shrine in secret grace.

In murmured code, the spheres entwine,
Revealing paths through ageless time,
Through ciphered verse and hidden line,
The cosmos doth its sign define.

Ye heed the stars, their dance aligned,
The secrets of the past enshrined,
With hearts aflame and souls set free,
The truth unfolds, as thee shall see.

'Shakespeare-style poetry? Not easy.' Emma said. Her ambitions quickly wilted as she realized deciphering the poetry was no piece of cake. 'Anyone got a Shakespearean English to Modern English dictionary stashed away in their backpacks?' she asked with a hint of desperation.

'Nobody brought one; I'm sure of it,' Adam reassured her.

'I don't even think a Shakespearean English to Modern English dictionary is a thing,' Aunt Mary chimed in, dismissing the concept entirely.

'Why don't you check whether there are any other useful parchments?' Adam suggested Emma.

'I suggest that we gather up all the parchments and the fancy iron gall ink, just in case there is microscopic information waiting for us.' Aunt Mary said.

'Sure, we could give that a shot, but let's first search these for *non-microscopic* wisdom,' Emma continued her search, carefully flipping through each parchment in the stack. Her fingers gently brushed over the aged pages as she carefully examined their contents.

After some time, just as hope was beginning to diminish, her eyes widened with excitement as she stumbled upon another parchment.

'I found another one, guys! Let's see what this parchment has to reveal.' Emma said

With excitement, they gathered around Emma as she began to read the newly discovered poetry, hoping for more clues and insights.

This was the poetry:

Beneath celestial cryptic gleam,

In hidden Records' cryptic scheme,

A cosmic lock, secrets bide,

A path out where wisdom hides.

The hieroglyphs, in riddles spun,
Their puzzled dance, by hopes begun,
Gazed the sky with hopes of light,
A celestial key, their quest invites.

'Oh, No. I never saw this coming.' Adam seemed terrified.

'What?' Emma couldn't contain her curiosity.

'The exit. 'A path out where wisdom hides."

Emma was still puzzled. 'And? What does that even mean?'

'The Hall of Records is "*where wisdom hides.*" "*Path out*" refers to the exit.'

'So?'

'We got in, but how do we get out? We don't wanna go out through the maze again. Do we?' Adam explained.

Emma realized. She understood what Adam was trying to say. 'So, we have to search everywhere and try to find a hieroglyph just to get out? It's like we're trapped.'

'We *would* be trapped if we didn't have the hieroglyph dictionary.'

'Well, thank that Latin to hieroglyph dictionary, then, although I would be happier with the Shakespearean English to Modern English dictionary,' Emma said with a sigh of relief.

'First thing's first. Let me help you with Shakespeare-style poetry. I loved reading Shakespeare's poems when I was a kid.' Aunt Mary said.

'Okay then, tell me what the first stanza means,' Emma asked Aunt Mary in a demanding voice.

'*When that table has been beautifully arranged,*
A tapestry in heavenly space,
A cosmic dance in the sky,
Hidden secrets with opportunity of wisdom.
This must be the modern English translation.'

'Okay, now what does that mean?'

'That's up to us,' Adam said.

'"*When the table has been arranged.*" What table? How on earth are we supposed to know what table it is? There are millions of tables all over the world.' Emma said with haste.

'First, calm down. Good. Now, coming to the point, I think we are talking about arranging the *periodic* table we saw. Remember zinc was missing?' said Adam the Calm.

'So, if we find zinc and place it in the empty box, there will be a dance show in the sky?'

'Ha!' Adam leaned back, deep in thought, and then burst into a laugh. 'A dance show in the sky? I don't think it will happen, but if it does, that would be a sight, wouldn't it?'

Aunt Mary chuckled. 'Well, I doubt the periodic table has plans for a dance show...'

'Yeah. But let's see what the next stanza holds!'

'Sure!

At the end of the next day,
The start will align and will gently sway,
Above the territory of Empire Zinc,
A secret shrine will get revealed.'

'Empire Zinc? Never heard of it.' Emma squinted at the parchment. 'Sounds like a cheap action movie title, doesn't it?'

Adam nodded, trying to contain his laughter. 'Totally! Starring Zinc Man, fighting villains with his rustproof shield!'

Aunt Mary chimed in, 'Well, let's focus on our own zinc mission.'

'Yeah. So, till now, I can say that we must arrange the periodic table, and we will have time until the end of the next day to exit the hall and find the Zinc Empire.' Adam theorized. 'Next stanza.'

'*In murmured code, the spheres tangle,*
Revealing a path through endless time,
To a coded verse with a hidden line,
The cosmos defines its sign.'

'"*Spheres*" could refer to the stars, right?' Emma asked.

'Could be. The rest of the lines tell us what we may find in the shrine. We can stop here. We'll look at the rest when we reach the shrine.'

'This is what we can do. First, we'll find the exit. Then, right before exiting, we will place the zinc. Then, we can ask historians about the Zinc Empire. This will save us time, as we have time only until the end of the next day.' Emma recommended

'That's a great strategy. But now we have to find the lock which contains the hieroglyphs.'

Exiting the Hall of Records had its own set of challenges and mysteries. They began to search for a way out. The exit, however, was not readily apparent.

They searched for hours but never found any sign of a lock or hieroglyph.

Emma, with her resourceful nature, was the first to notice an unusual pattern in the floor's tiles. And no, the unusual pattern wasn't the hieroglyph.

'Adam, do you see that?' She asked, carefully observing the tile.

'What is it?'

'The floor tiles'

'Right! Now that you say it, I see it.'

What Emma had discovered was a pattern that didn't quite match the rest of the chamber. Upon closer inspection, they found that one of the tiles, when pressed, revealed a hidden compartment. Within the compartment was an intricate mechanism adorned with a short hieroglyph.

'I think we'll have to go through a less painstaking process than the previous hieroglyph to decode this,' Adam said with a sigh.

'There were seven different letters in the previous one, right?' Emma asked.

'I don't remember, but this one obviously has fewer letters than the previous one.'

The hieroglyph was something like this:

'This looks familiar.' Emma seemed to realize something. 'Hmm. This is the same hieroglyph as the first word of the previous hieroglyph.'

'You mean 'east'?'

'Yeah. Let's search toward the east.'

'Good thing I've got a compass in my bag,' Adam said, taking out a compass from his bag.

'That way. It's east.' Adam said, pointing to his left.

The three walked confidently toward the east, hoping to find an exit.

Their footsteps echoed through the dimly lit corridor as they walked towards the east, guided by the hieroglyph's clue. It felt like a journey through time itself, surrounded by ancient knowledge and mysteries.

As they went deeper into the chamber's eastern passage, Emma suddenly halted. She pointed to the wall on her left. 'What's this?'

There, another inscription revealed itself, partially obscured by dust. This one represented an alignment of stars and planets.

'Looks like we're on the right track,' Adam remarked, gazing at the inscription.

'It looks interesting...'

'This appears to be a map of a certain constellation with a specific alignment. It must be part of the clue.'

Aunt Mary sifted through the celestial pattern. 'It's like a '*cosmic dance*,' isn't it? Just like the first stanza of the poetry. A clue within a clue, perhaps?'

'But then, wasn't the poetry about the Zinc Empire?' Emma felt confused.

Adam replied, 'Hmm... The two poems we found might be connected. Also, both of them were found in the same place, which explains a part of it. After we unlock the exit, we'll have to quickly go back to the periodic table and place the zinc. Wait, where do we get the zinc?'

'We can go out, get the zinc, come back in, and place the zinc. Simple!' Emma said.

'What if the exit is one way? Then, if we get out, we won't be able to get in.'

'Then we'll have to search for zinc in the hall itself.'

Aunt Mary said after trying to recall something. 'I remember seeing an iron nail. It must have been coated with zinc, or else it would have easily rusted.'

'Okay. So, we scrape the zinc and place it. Good. Now, let's look at this inscription.'

With renewed determination, they continued along the corridor, now watching the stars and planets depicted on the walls. They knew they were on the right track but needed to interpret the clues correctly.

'Alright, folks, I've got an idea. Let's sketch the arrangement of stars and planets in that inscription. I've got a good eye for details, so I think I can get this down.'

Saying so, Adam pulled out a piece of paper and sketched the arrangement of stars and planets as they appeared in the inscription. His keen eyes were able to spot perfectly positioned dots.

The three of them began to examine the floor and the walls for any hidden mechanisms or symbols related to this celestial event. Their eyes kept a close watch on the walls, floors, and ceiling of the chamber for any signs that would lead them to the exit.

As they searched, Aunt Mary noticed a slight depression on the floor that seemed different from the rest of the tiles. She knelt down and gently pressed it. With a soft click, a section of the wall adjacent to them slid open, revealing a narrow passageway.

'This is it,' Adam said, his heart racing. 'The path to the exit.'

'Huh? Another corridor? I thought that this was the exit!' Emma was impatient and wanted to find the exit right away.

'I guess the architects did not wanna make it easy to either enter or escape,' Adam said with a smile.

With a newfound sense of urgency, they entered the passageway. It was dark, and their footsteps echoed as they walked deeper into the unknown. They felt the weight of their quest on their shoulders, the knowledge that they were close to uncovering ancient secrets.

After what seemed like an eternity, the passage led them to a circular chamber. In the center, a large, ornate door stood, adorned with hieroglyphs and symbols that glistened in the torchlight.

'This must be the exit,' Aunt Mary said. 'We're almost there.'

The door's inscription revealed a code, a riddle of sorts. The answer, they hoped, would lead them to the other side.

This is what was inscribed on the door:

- --- / ..-. .. -. -.. / - .... . / . -..- .. - / -.-. --
- ... -- .. -.-. / .- -. -.. / .-- .. -.. . / .-- .. - ....
/ ... - .- .-. ... / .- .-.. .. --. -. . -.. / .- -. -.. / .-
- .. ... -.. --- -- / .- ... / --- ..- .-. / --. ..- .. -.. .
/ .- / -.-. . .-.. . ... - .. .- .-.. / -.. .- -. -.-. . / ..
-. / - .... . / .... . .- ...- . -. ... / .-- . / - .-. .-
-.-. . / .. -. / - .... . / -.- -. --- .-- .-.. . -.. --. .
/ .-- . / ... . . -.- / .-- . / ..-. .. -. -.. / --- ..- .-.
/ . -- -... .-. .- -.-. .

'What's this? Dots again?' Emma, as usual, was confused with codes.'

'This is obviously Morse code. You've never heard of it?' Adam said.

'I know Morse. It's the code used by lighthouses to communicate, usually with aircraft and ships.' Aunt Mary revealed one of her other talents.

With anticipation building, Aunt Mary took Adam's notebook and started deciphering the code. After a few minutes, Aunt Mary ended up with a poetic riddle:

TO FIND THE EXIT COSMIC AND WIDE,
WITH STARS ALIGNED AND WISDOM AS OUR GUIDE,
A CELESTIAL DANCE IN THE HEAVENS WE TRACE,
IN THE KNOWLEDGE WE SEEK, WE FIND OUR EMBRACE.

Aunt Mary nodded in understanding. 'It's clear now. See the lock?'

'Yeah'

'We need to recreate the celestial alignment, indicated in the previous inscription, on the lock to open the door.'

'Let's use the constellation Adam mapped from the wall,' Emma suggested. 'If we align the stars and planets just as they appear, the door must open.'

They looked at the constellation they had sketched earlier, carefully noting the positions of each star.

With their collective efforts, they began to arrange the levers on the lock in a way that mimicked the celestial dance depicted in the inscription.

As the last lever was positioned, they held their breath, waiting for something to happen.

Suddenly, the ornate door began to rumble and slowly swung open, revealing a ray of sunlight.

'The door is open!' Emma exclaimed. Her voice was filled with excitement.

Adam told Aunt Mary, 'Take the iron nail you saw and go to the periodic table. Use the tungsten to scrape off the zinc. Place the zinc and tungsten back. Come back as soon as you can. We can't be sure whether the door will remain open for long.'

'Sure.'

Aunt Mary did what Adam said. It did take some time to scrape the zinc, as tungsten was challenging but not that sharp. She placed the zinc and tungsten. She knew something was happening at the ruins of the Zinc Empire. She ran as fast as she could towards the exit.

Adam and Emma were waiting for her. As soon as she came, they stepped out, and they finally took a breath of fresh air after a pretty long time.

Chapter 8
The Mysterious Empire

The siblings emerged from the Hall of Records, driven by a newfound sense of purpose and urgency.

They knew they had to locate the Zinc Empire to unlock the secrets hidden within the shrine. Remember how they came out of a 'door'? Yeah. They did. But then, when they exited the door, something happened. The door? It was gone, just as Adam predicted.

Well, I know that the door isn't important now, but it seemed like it was something significant when Emma turned back and asked with curiosity, 'Where's the door?'

Adam replied to her question, 'My predictions were accurate then. It was a one-way door.'

'It was one-way for a reason. If it was not, then anyone could have gotten in without going through the maze, right?' Aunt Mary said.

'Yeah. And I don't think we have time to waste. We'll have to find a historian.'

'And... where do we find one?'

'Let's just search. I'm sure we'll find one.'

As they stepped out further into the daylight, Emma's memory brought forth a faint recollection. She remembered a man, the same one who had pointed them to the Karnak Temple and the legend of Alexander the Great.

'Guys, I think I know someone who can help us find the Zinc Empire,' Emma shared her revelation.

'Who?' Adam asked.

'Remember the man who told us about the Karnak Temple and guided us toward the legend of Anthony the Great? We could go back there and ask him for directions.'

'You mean the one who was speaking Arabic?'

'Yeah.'

'But won't we need another translator?'

'We'll find one, or we could go back to Anthony himself.'

'Nah. That'll be a long walk in the Karnak temple.'

Adam and Aunt Mary agreed, and they made their way back to where they found that person. However, after walking for some time, they began to realize that something was amiss. The landscape around them looked unfamiliar, and the landmarks they had expected were nowhere to be seen.

After a while, Emma spoke up. 'Does something feel off to you?'

'Hmm... You're right. We should have reached The Sphinx by now, but everything seems different,' Aunt Mary observed, her brows furrowing in confusion.

Adam chimed in, 'And the landscape seems different too. It's as if we're in a completely different place.'

'Emma, are you sure this is the right way?' Aunt Mary asked.

'I'm positive. I'm trying to recall the path we took underground to reach back to The Sphinx. Emma replied, her voice tinged with doubt. 'But it's like we've entered a whole new part of the Sahara.'

The siblings decided to continue walking, hoping to find someone who could provide directions.

They walked for hours, trying to find a populated place.

'Firstly, I don't think there is any population here. And secondly, the clock is ticking.' Emma said

'What clock?' said Adam the Forgetful.

'You don't remember? We have time only until the end of tomorrow to find the Zinc Empire.'

'Ahh... Now I remember. But then, what if we don't reach on time? Will the shrine not open?' Adam thought for a while.

'It may. It may not. The poem doesn't say anything about it.'

After a while, they encountered a small settlement, a stark contrast to the barren landscape that surrounded it.

'Finally!' Emma said with a sigh.

'How do they even live here? Lack of water, no proper education, and hospitals...' Adam was surprised.

'Small huts, too,' Emma added on.

Aunt Mary spoke, 'At least we found something. If there was no population, then we would have probably walked in the wrong direction...'

'...and reached the bay,' Emma continued.

'Ha!'

Finally, they came upon a small settlement. Eager to find out where they were, Emma approached a local resident and asked, 'Excuse me, can you tell us where we are?'

The resident spoke rapidly in a language the siblings couldn't understand. Their expressions conveyed confusion, and it was evident they couldn't comprehend English.

'We don't seem to understand their language, do we?' Emma said in frustration.

'They could be speaking Arabic. Common people of Egypt seem to be speaking Arabic.'

'I don't think we are in Egypt.'

Aunt Mary, who had been listening closely, suddenly recognized the language. 'Ahh. I believe they're speaking Spanish. I know a bit of Spanish. Let me give it a try.'

'You-Did-Not-Tell-Us-Before. Why?' Emma was frustrated as she got hold of another secret from Aunt Mary.

'Emma, chill. Let's just be happy that we have a translator. Imagine none of us knew Spanish. We would be stuck here!'

'Fine!'

Aunt Mary initiated a conversation with the locals, addressing them in Spanish. With her translation skills, she was able to understand their responses.

Aunt Mary said, '*Hablas Español?*'

To their surprise, the residents responded in Spanish. Aunt Mary carried on a brief conversation.

'*Hola. ¿Podrías decirnos qué lugar es este?*' Aunt Mary asked in Spanish.

'*Somos la tribu saharaui. Estás en el Sahara occidental.*'

'No, this is not possible.' Aunt Mary was surprised.

'What is it?'

'They say we are in Western Sahara,' Aunt Mary relayed the information.

'How? We can't be traveling through time and space that fast!'

'Time, Huh? Let me ask them what day it is. Could you tell us today's date?' Aunt Mary asked in Spanish.

'*Pero es Marzo de dos mil cuatro.*'

'Impossible. There is no way the Ancient Egyptians could time travel.'

'Now what?'

'They say it's the year 2004.' Aunt Mary relayed the information.

'2004?' Emma gasped. 'That means we've lost an entire year! We should be back in 2003.'

'Time seems to have passed quite differently inside the Hall of Records.'

Adam, however, was persistent. 'That's a year of school and normal life that we've missed, but we're here for a reason. Let's find a historian who can help us learn about the Zinc Empire. We can't afford to waste any more time.'

'*¿Conoces a un historiador que pueda hablar inglés?*' Aunt Mary asked the local resident.

'*Si*'

'*Seguro. llévanos allí*' Aunt Mary said to the resident.

The resident replied, and Aunt Mary said, 'We'll have to travel on a camel cart.'

'Fun!' Emma was excited, as it was their first time on a camel cart.

After a few hours, they stopped at a small hut. They knocked on the door.

'Hello, how may I help you?'

'We need the assistance of a historian.'

'Sure. Come in.'

The siblings found themselves in a small, dusty room surrounded by books and artifacts.

'What information do you need?'

'We're looking for information about the Zinc Empire,' Emma explained to the historian.

The historian listened attentively, but when Emma mentioned the Zinc Empire, his brow furrowed. 'I'm sorry, but I've never come across any historical reference to the Zinc Empire. It doesn't exist in any of our records.'

'I'm confident that it exists,' Adam responded.

The siblings felt disheartened, but the historian continued, 'However, I have a colleague in Morocco who specializes in ancient civilizations. He might be able to help you better. Let me arrange a meeting for you.'

The siblings decided to follow the historian's recommendation. He provided them with contact information, and Aunt Mary arranged for their transportation to Morocco by helicopter.

As the helicopter to Morocco arrived, they boarded it.

'Thanks for your assistance.' Aunt Mary said as they left.

After a long flight of several minutes, the helicopter landed at a very luxurious house in Morocco. It was already night, and they had around 24 hours left.

'This does not look like a historian's house,' Emma said.

'Yeah. I expected it to be like my uncle's study. Like some archaeological sites.'

'I think that's because you're looking at the wrong house...' The historian said: '*That* is my friend's house,' he said, pointing at a house in a totally different direction.

'Oh. Now it makes sense.' Adam understood.

'But that is still not what I expected,' Emma said.

'Hmm... A historian's workstation may be full of scrolls and copies of ancient texts, but that doesn't mean that their whole house will look like an archaeological site.' The historian explained.

The historian took them to his friend's house. He introduced his friend as Robert.

The historian introduced Adam, Emma, and Aunt Mary to Robert.

'Do you happen to know anything about the Zinc Empire?' Emma started a conversation.

'Zinc Empire?' Robert thought for a while. 'Are you sure it is the Zinc Empire? I've never heard of it.'

The siblings were disheartened when Robert continued, 'But there could have been a misunderstanding. There is no record of a Zinc Empire, but there are mentions of ruins associated with an unexplored civilization known as the Zingh Empire.'

'Do you know where it is located?' Adam asked.

'The best landmark would be the Algerian Megaliths.'

'We need to go there,' Emma asked Aunt Mary to arrange a flight.

'I could help in arranging a copter. I could also accompany you.

Robert offered to take them to the location of the Zingh Empire's alleged ruins in Algeria.

After a quick flight, they arrived in Algeria.

'We are in Algeria,' Robert remarked.

'This place does not look barren to me,' Emma said as the helicopter started descending.

'Yeah. This place is well populated.' Adam added on.

'Just wait until we land.'

Robert was right. As they traveled further, they were able to see a hilly, unpopulated land with several pyramid-like structures.

As they landed, Robert spoke, 'We are here at the destination. The Algerian megaliths. There are thirteen burial sites. Most of them are unexplored.'

'So, these are burial sites of the Zingh Empire, right?' Adam asked.

'No one can say for sure. Most people believe it is a burial site of the Berber civilization, but some archaeologists say that they are of the Zingh Empire.

As they stepped out, they went further into the desert.

As they walked among the ancient stones, a sense of wonder and hope filled the air. The Algerian Megaliths were evidence of a lost civilization, a civilization that might have answers to their most profound questions.

'I'll leave you here. Continue your journey.' Robert said. 'And, take this.' Robert handed Aunt Mary a button. 'Press the button when you want to go back to Morocco. I'll send a flight.'

'Thank you.'

As Robert left, Emma looked around, her eyes sparkling with determination. 'We're one step closer to uncovering the truth about Mom and Dad. Let's see what secrets this place has in store for us.'

They couldn't help but feel they were on the brink of a monumental discovery as they went deeper into the megaliths. Their quest for knowledge and their pursuit of answers to the mysteries of the past had brought them to this point, and they were ready to embrace whatever revelations lay ahead.

The megaliths stood in silence, holding the weight of centuries of history, ready to reveal the secrets hidden within their ancient stones.

Emma stopped. She seemed to realize something. 'We forgot what we were here for. We were not here to search the megaliths. Were we?'

Aunt Mary realized that, too. 'You're right. We were not here for the megaliths. We were here for the shrine.'

Adam seemed to realize this too. 'Yeah, but we'll have to wait for the celestial dance, right? So, we have nothing to do other than wait until night falls.'

'Well, both of you are right. We do have to wait until night falls, but we also have to keep a look at the sky and not miss the celestial dance. If we do miss it, the shrine may not reveal itself.'

'Where do you think the celestial dance will occur?' Emma asked.

'Aunt, could you reread the poem?'

'Let me see...

When yon table's loom hath woven grace,

A tapestry in heavenly space...'

'No Archaic English, please.'

'Okay.

When that table has been beautifully arranged,

A tapestry in heavenly space,

A cosmic dance in the sky,

Hidden secrets with an opportunity of wisdom...'

'Wait. What tapestry is it talking about?' Emma pointed out. 'If we find the tapestry, we may be able to locate the cosmic dance.'

'"*A tapestry in heavenly space*" ... If it is in space, then it might be referring to a constellation...'

'...which looks like a tapestry,' Emma continued.

'Right. But I have never heard about a constellation that looks like a tapestry. We can resolve this matter later on. Aunt, could you continue?'

'*At the end of the next day,*

The start will align and will gently sway,

Above the territory of Empire Zinc,

A secret shrine will be revealed.

In murmured code, the spheres tangle...'

'Spheres. We thought them to be planets or stars, but what about the murmured code? Emma said.

'What code is a code you can hear and decode?' Adam asked.

'I don't know.'

'What about Morse? You can hear it, note it, and decode it.' Aunt Mary answered.

'Yeah. I think 'murmured code' refers to Morse code.'

'Isn't Morse code dots and dashes? How can you hear it?' Emma seemed confused, as she knew Morse code as only dots and dashes.

'In Morse code, a short beep is a dot, and a long beep is a dash. A long gap refers to a space.' Aunt Mary explained.

'Hmm... So, are you trying to say that the spheres are not stars and planets but the dots in Morse code?'

'Seems so,' Adam replied.

'But then, how can the dots tangle? If it were the dashes tangling, it's understandable.'

'Metaphors, hyperboles... This is a poem, Emma. Haven't you learned about poetic devices?'

'Nah. Who pays attention to English classes? By the way, we only learned about similes, and I think the teacher said something about metaphors...'

'Okay, forget it. I think tangle refers to getting jumbled. Remember the door lock that had dots on the levers?'

'Finally. You remember something. And yeah, I remember the dots on the levers.'

'They were jumbled. We had to place them in the right order. We might encounter something similar.' Adam continued. 'I think this was all that the poem said about finding the shrine. Let's just wait for the cosmic dance.

Chapter 9
The Cosmic Dance

The sun dipped below the horizon, casting the Sahara in a warm, golden glow.

The siblings eagerly awaited the cosmic dance mentioned in the encoded poetry. The sky stretched above them, a vast canvas awaiting its celestial performance. Their imaginations ran wild as they wondered what this mysterious phenomenon would entail.

'What do you think the cosmic dance will look like?' Emma asked, her eyes fixed on the darkening heavens.

'Perhaps the stars will twinkle and arrange themselves into some pattern,' Adam speculated, also mesmerized by the darkening skies.

'*The stars, aligned, shall gently sway*,' Aunt Mary reminded them. 'I believe we're about to witness the stars align and sway, as described in the poem.'

Adam and Emma nodded in agreement and continued to gaze skyward, eager to witness the cosmic dance. When the siblings looked at her, they noticed that she was not gazing at the sky like them, but she was gazing at something else on land. Adam and Emma exchanged glances.

'What's got your attention?' Adam asked, curious about her distraction.

'Who, me?' Aunt Mary replied, still gazing at the sight before her.

'Yes, you. What are you looking at?'

Aunt Mary finally shifted her gaze from the ground to her bewildered companions. 'Can't you see that?'

'See what?' Emma inquired.

'The sand vortex.'

'Isn't that just a result of the wind? There's wind everywhere.' Adam inquired, checking their surroundings for further evidence.

Aunt Mary shook her head. 'I don't think so. Take a look around.' She paused for a while. 'Do you see any other sand vortexes?'

Adam looked around. 'No, I don't see any.'

The sand vortex, a slowly swirling, pillar-like conical formation, seemed to rise higher into the night sky, growing more significant and more distinct.

It had an incomprehensible and eerie quality, unlike anything the siblings had ever encountered.

'Do you feel that?' Emma questioned as she drew deep breaths. 'It's like the air is thinning, and there's less oxygen.'

Adam nodded in agreement, his brows furrowing. 'I feel it, too. This is bizarre.'

As Adam drew closer to the sand vortex, he noticed something unusual. 'Guys, come take a look at this. The sand is appearing out of thin air.'

'I thought you said that the wind was causing the sand to form a vortex,' Aunt Mary questioned.

'The vortex might be caused by wind, but the sand particles themselves are seemingly appearing from nowhere. This is not possible. Is it?'

The siblings continued to watch in astonishment as the sand vortex swirled higher, reaching further into the night sky. They gradually comprehended that the sand being drawn up was not ordinary sand; it was composed of tiny, glistening pieces of quartz.

Adam observed what was happening. 'This is quartz? Sand is quartz?' He said as he noticed that the sand was emerging from pieces of quartz.

'This is quartz sand,' Aunt Mary remarked as she observed the emerging particles. 'It's made up of minute fragments of quartz. Makes sense.'

'Wow! I never knew there was something called quartz sand.' Adam said.

'Quartz sand's nothing new. Quartz is the most common source of sand.'

Just then, Emma noticed something. 'There! The cosmic dance. It's starting!'

She was indeed right. The sand vortex ascended to touch the starry canopy. The sand vortex seemed to touch the sky and rearrange the stars. The stars above them started to arrange themselves into intricate and mesmerizing patterns. The siblings watched in absolute wonder as the stars created a stunning celestial tapestry, just like the one described in Shakespeare-style poetry.

'A *tapestry in heavenly space*,' Aunt Mary murmured with reverence. 'It's a magnificent celestial tapestry.'

As the cosmic spectacle unfolded above, the vortex of quartz sand eventually dispersed and scattered, revealing an enigmatic door hidden beneath the ephemeral sands.

'This must be the entrance to the shrine,' Adam declared with exhilaration, moving closer to examine it.

The stars' glow covered the door's surface in an intricate pattern, the very same one that decorated the night sky above.

'Adam, look at this.'

'The pattern?

'Yeah. The rays from the stars are in perfect alignment with the dots on the entrance.'

Adam studied the alignment and realized that not all the celestial dots corresponded precisely with the door's pattern.

'I see. But not all are in line.'

'Right! They must be the 'tangled spheres' that were mentioned in the poetry.'

'Hmm... Can I move these carved dots?' Adam said as he tried to manipulate one of the dots.

To his surprise, the dot responded to his touch, allowing itself to be moved into the proper alignment.

'Perhaps,' Aunt Mary chimed in, her voice filled with excitement, 'if we can align all the dots according to the pattern in which the stars are arranged, the door will open.'

Determined and focused, the three of them set to work aligning each of the dots on the door. As they synchronized the last one, the ancient mechanism responded, and the massive stone entrance began to shift and creak open.

They marveled at the intricate connection between astronomy and mechanics, the wisdom of the past that had blended the cosmic and the terrestrial.

'How were the ancient civilizations capable of connecting astronomy and mechanics?' Emma asked.

'Forget that. How did the ancient civilizations even *know* mechanical engineering?' Adam added on.

'Throughout our journey, we've encountered a plethora of evidence suggesting that our ancestors possessed knowledge far beyond our own. Consider this: have you ever imagined that we could manipulate the stars?'

'Well, we're often fixated on reaching the stars, channeling our efforts into building complex technology like rockets. Yet, in contrast, it seems our ancestors pursued a different, more mystical connection with the stars.' Adam replied.

'Okay, then. Do we jump in?' Emma asked

'I don't know. It looks pretty deep.' Adam replied.

'Well, I know it's deep. But my question was, '*Do we jump in?*'' Emma said, this time in a louder voice.

'We could drop something.'

'And then?'

'If we drop something heavy, we can say how deep it is by checking how long it takes for it to fall.

'That's a good idea, but what do we have that we can drop?'

'I wish we had a rock.'

'We could search for one.'

Just then, they heard a sizzling sound. Something was burning. After a while, it was no longer heard.

'Did you hear that?' Emma asked.

'Yeah,' Adam replied, looking around.

'Hey, where did this come from?' Aunt Mary chimed in.

'What is it?' Adam asked curiously.

'It's a rock.'

Adam and Emma exchanged glances. They were just talking about searching for a rock.

Adam examined the rock carefully. 'This looks like a meteorite. This is what must have been the sizzling sound.'

'How can a meteor crash be so perfectly timed?'

'I don't know. Also, there is no way there is only one meteorite. They usually fall as meteorite showers.'

'Let's just check whether we can jump in or not,' Emma suggested.

Adam dropped the meteorite. It was only after a few minutes that they sensed the meteorite fall.

'Good thing we didn't jump in blindly. If we had, then we would have been dead by now.'

'Whatever. Now, how do we get there?'

'No idea. I wish that this wasn't so complicated to get into.'

Suddenly, as they stared into the deep pit, they heard a sound from inside.

'What's that? It's come from inside the shrine, right?'

'It sounds like a mechanical shift in something.'

After a while, Emma spoke. 'Adam, do you remember the Valley of Knowledge?'

'That's...like a year ago, right?'

'You forgot. Didn't you?'

'I don't remember much.'

'I think this place has something in common with the valley of knowledge. Remember how the Valley of Knowledge responded to our wishes?'

'Yeah.'

'This place is doing the same. You wished for a rock, and we got a meteorite.'

'I get it. So... when I wished for the entrance to be less complicated, something must have changed to let us go in easily.'

Adam looked around and observed the entrance. He noticed that he was able to step into the entrance. 'This is what has changed. It's a staircase.'

The staircase made their work easier. They walked into the entrance. As they went deeper into the shrine, the light started dimming.

'It's getting darker,' Emma said

'I know. I can't even see anything,' Adam replied.

'Same here.'

'Why not wish for light? You do it this time.'

'Let's see. I wish that this place was lit.'

They waited. Nothing seemed to have happened.

'Try again.'

'I wish for light,' Emma repeated. 'Ahh...this is really heavy.'

'What's heavy?'

'I think it's the meteorite that we dropped.'

'How can that have to do something with light?'

Aunt Mary was listening. 'It could be a key to light.'

'If that's the key, then where is the lock?' Adam asked.

'I think it's right behind me.'

'Behind you? Why didn't you tell us about it all this time?' Emma exclaimed.

'It's fine. Now, where is the lock?'

'Here. It's like a socket for the meteorite.' Aunt Mary pointed towards the socket, although nobody could see each other. But luckily, Adam was able to feel the socket with his hands.

'Emma, I found the socket. Give me the meteorite.'

Adam was able to take the meteorite from Emma and place it in the socket.

'It fits perfectly,' Adam mentioned.

After a while, they could see light.

'I see the light!' Emma said.

'But where is the light coming from?'

'I think it is a torch.'

'You're right. There are torches everywhere.'

'Now that we can see our surroundings, what do you think we're gonna find here?' Emma asked.

'That brings us to the rest of the poem,' Adam said. 'Aunt, could you read the rest of the poem? From the third stanza.'

'Sure

In murmured code the spheres tangle,
Revealing a path through endless time,
To a coded verse with a hidden line,
The cosmos defines its sign.'

'Wait. If the path revealed is through "*endless time,*" does that mean time is endless here?' Emma asked.

'Isn't time always endless?' Adam pointed out.

'Oh. Right.'

'So, if we consider "*endless*" as an adjective, eliminating it won't affect the meaning.'

'So, are you trying to say we are on a "*path that goes through time*"?'

'Yes, and it means that time may go faster or slower than normal. Coming to the next line, "*To a coded verse with a hidden line*," ...I think it clearly says that we will find a coded poem with a missing line.'

'What about the next line, "*The cosmos defines its sign.*"?'

'It could be talking about a mark that the universe will leave on the Earth. I can't say for sure. Okay. Let's hear the next part.'

'*You heed the stars, their dance aligned,*
The secrets of the past enshrined,
With hearts aflame and souls set free,
The truth unfolds, as you shall see.'

'There's nothing much in this one, right?' Emma asked

'There is.'

'What's there? There's nothing. We've already heeded stars...'

'The third line,' Adam interrupted.

Emma thought about the third line for a while. She seemed to understand what Adam meant. 'I see.

'*With hearts aflame'*... Who would be cruel enough to set a heart on flames?'

'Woah! 'aflame' doesn't always mean setting on fire.'

'Then what?'

'This is another metaphor. Look at the previous line. '*The secrets of the past enshrined*' It says that the secrets are '*enshrined*' or, more like, '*trapped*' in this case. At the end of the next line, it says, 'souls set free.' The souls must be the secrets... Or are the secrets the soul?' Adam thought deeply for a while.

'What struck you?'

'I think I was wrong all this time. We are not searching for clues as objects but as people.'

'People? So, you are telling me that we are gonna meet a person in *this* underground shrine?'

'Don't act like it's the first time. We've already met Anthony, the monk, who was hiding in the Karnak temple.'

'Yeah, I know,' Emma replied.

'Do you think that we should move forward without wasting time?' Aunt Mary said as she lost her patience.

'She's right. We should not waste time here, as time may run faster here.' Adam agreed.

The three of them walked further. In the shrine, they found an array of ancient artifacts and documents preserved within meticulously carved stone chambers. These chambers appeared to be a repository of knowledge, spanning various fields of study. They discovered several things.

'Hey! Look at that chart,' Emma said, pointing to charts mapping the observable universe with incredible precision, hinting at an in-depth understanding of celestial bodies, including stars, planets, and constellations.

'That's...the whole universe. I think it has more information than whatever NASA has discovered till now.' Adam added on.

'This place is like the Hall of Records, but better.'

'Why don't we carry these? They will be useful for today's archaeologists and scientists.'

'You could do that, but make sure not to trigger any traps,' Adam warned.

Luckily, picking up the chart did not trigger any traps but revealed manuscripts containing detailed instructions for creating elixirs, transmuting substances, and mastering the art of alchemy.

'Should I take these? I think these elixirs will help save lives.'

'It's up to you.'

Again, no traps were triggered. 'See! I don't trigger traps.'

After walking further, they found scrolls filled with advanced mathematical concepts, including calculus, algebra, and even geometry topics like trigonometry, which showcased their profound grasp of mathematics.

They also found ancient medical texts that explored remedies, herbal treatments, and even surgical techniques, revealing a profound knowledge of ancient medicine. Aunt Mary obviously took them.

'Adam! Look at those scrolls.' Emma pointed at a cryptic scroll.

'That looks like it's encoded with riddles, hidden messages, and clues.'

'I'll go and take it.' Aunt Mary said.

'Again, be careful not to trigger any trap.' Adam seemed to be really careful about traps.

Aunt Mary went and picked up the scroll, which hinted at more discoveries yet to be made.

As they ventured deeper into the shrine, they were captivated by the wisdom of a civilization that had long since disappeared, marveling at the depth of knowledge held within its stone walls. The shrine offered the promise of unraveling the mysteries of life, the universe, and the secrets that bound them all.

Chapter 10
The Enshrined Secret

The siblings, guided by the shadowy poem, ventured deeper into the corridors of the underground shrine.

Their footsteps echoed in the dimly lit passages. The walls were adorned with beautiful carvings and relics from ages long past.

Dust and time had combined to create an ancient atmosphere that seemed to teleport them to a different era. I mean, really. It was like they were in a time machine.

The debate about the identity of the mysterious person they were about to meet had been a lively one.

They walked deeper into the heart of the underground. Emma couldn't help but ponder the connection between this place and the Zingh Empire.

'I have a feeling the person we're gonna meet is somehow connected to the Zingh Empire,' she started a conversation, her eyes filled with intrigue.

'Considering the reference in the poetry, it would make sense, right?'

Adam, being the analytical thinker in the group, took a different approach. He was thinking about the Shakespearean-style poem that had led them here. 'It's possible,' he began, considering Emma's theory. 'But think about it, Emma. The shrine guided us here using a poem in the style of Shakespeare. What if the person we meet is related to Shakespeare in some way? It could be a playwright, scholar, or even Shakespeare himself. Maybe Shakespeare knew this place, and his words guided us here.'

The siblings' debate continued to echo through the dimly lit corridors of the underground shrine. With each footstep, they went deeper into the chronicles of history.

Emma, whose imagination was set ablaze by the mysteries that surrounded them, couldn't help but revisit the connection to the Zingh Empire.

Her voice held a hint of excitement as she voiced her thoughts. 'I still can't get over the Zingh Empire reference. It feels like we're on the brink of uncovering something truly remarkable, something that could rewrite the history books.'

Adam, ever the pragmatic thinker, pondered her theory. 'It's an intriguing connection, no doubt. But we should remain open to other possibilities.

Remember, these ancient places often have multiple layers of history and meaning. Perhaps the Zingh Empire was just one of many influences on this shrine.'

Aunt Mary, walking a few steps behind the siblings, listened to their debate with keen interest. 'What's important is that we stay focused on our goal–uncovering the secrets this place holds. The truth might be stranger than we imagine.' Aunt Mary said, not wanting to waste time on a debate, which was totally unnecessary, as they were going to know whom they were going to meet in a while.

As they continued down the corridor, the dim light revealed even more beautiful carvings and artifacts, each telling a story of a forgotten time. The walls seemed to whisper secrets, and the artifacts summoned a sense of admiration for the people who had walked these paths long before.

The debate carried on. The hushed voices of the siblings... well, it was like a symphony of curiosity and wonder. Every carving and artifact they encountered seemed to add a new note to the melody of their thoughts.

Then, as they ventured deeper into the labyrinth, the mysterious voice once again called out from the shadows, interrupting their debate.

'Ποιος είσαι και γιατί είσαι εδώ;'

It was in a language neither Adam nor Emma were familiar with.

Confusion wrinkled their brows. Aunt Mary, however, recognized the language and promptly translated for the siblings. 'It is Greek. The voice is asking, 'Who are you, and why are you here?''

Emma asked, 'Do you know English?' She ventured, her curiosity getting the better of her. Last time, during their encounter with Anthony the Great, Aunt Mary spoke in Latin to him, but later, they found out that Anthony could speak English too. Emma didn't want something like that to happen again.

And just as she expected, the voice replied. 'I can speak in several languages, although I prefer Greek.'

Emma pressed on with her questions, puzzled by the mysterious entity that spoke from the darkness. 'How do you know English? That too, modern English.'

The unknown voice responded, 'I have been here for a very long time. I have witnessed the world change and languages evolve.'

'Now tell me who you are and why you are here.'

Aunt Mary introduced themselves and explained their presence in the shrine. 'I am Mary Wilson, and they are Adam and Emma. We are from America. We came here because Shakespearean-style poetry had guided us here.'

The voice was intrigued by their explanation. 'Shakespearean-style poetry? He wrote a poem about this place?'

Aunt Mary clarified, 'Not about this place itself, but a poem on finding and entering this place.'

The revelation seemed to pique the interest of the voice further. 'I may have an explanation. After me, Shakespeare was the one to find this place.'

Astonished by the mention of Shakespeare, the siblings exchanged a quick glance, realizing the historical significance of the person they were conversing with.

Aunt Mary continued to inquire, 'Has he been here?' The voice elaborated on its connection to Shakespeare. 'Yes... Now, coming back to our previous conversation, you do not know what you have come for, do you?

Their conversation had taken a curious turn. Adam decided to take his chances and engage further. 'We don't know exactly, but we do expect to find some ancient secrets.'

'Now that you know who we are and why we are here, can you show yourself so that we can talk face-to-face?' Emma asked as she was frustrated talking to an invisible voice.

The voice explained its limitations. 'I cannot show myself up to you, but I could guide you to me.'

Eager to meet the person behind the enigmatic voice, they accepted the offer.

'Then guide us. We need to see who we are speaking to.'

They continued to navigate the complex passageways, guided by the mysterious voice.

As they proceeded, the feeble glow of the torches cast eerie shadows on the walls, creating an even more ancient atmosphere. And I'll be honest, it was almost like the invisible voice had transported them to an entirely different realm.

While the journey through the shrine was punctuated with moments of confusion, anticipation, and curiosity, they continued to be guided by the mysterious voice.

Finally, they found themselves at the heart of the underground shrine, a place filled with a sense of splendor and history.

It was there, in the dimly lit chamber, that the mysterious figure they had been communicating with gradually emerged from the obscurity.

Their collective gasp was swallowed by the vastness of the underground chamber as a pharaoh, regal and imposing, emerged from the shadows.

The person before them was none other than Cleopatra the Seventh, one of the most iconic figures in history.

'A pharaoh? Impossible. Didn't pharaohs exist thousands of years ago?' Adam exclaimed, struggling to reconcile history with the extraordinary presence of Cleopatra.

Cleopatra regarded them with a mixture of curiosity and wisdom. The name struck a chord, echoing through the chronicles of history.

'Why are you here, Cleopatra?' Aunt Mary inquired, curious about the renowned historical figure's presence in the place.

Cleopatra began to share her remarkable tale, her voice carrying the weight of centuries. 'I found this place by chance, and I discovered its unique power—manipulation. By being near this place, I realized that I could manipulate nearly anything. I came here seeking a way to live forever by manipulating time. But the shrine punished me for my ambition by trapping me here for eternity. At first, it didn't seem like much, as I still *did* have the chance to live forever. But I do not want to be trapped forever, just to live forever.'

All of them listened intently, their expression changing from one of curiosity to understanding.

Adam's curiosity got the better of him, and he wanted to inquire further. 'Cleopatra, why were you imprisoned? What did the shrine consider your wrongdoing?'

Cleopatra responded with a mournful tone. 'The shrine punishes those who desire to use the power of manipulation for their own good, especially to escape death. It considered my quest for eternal life to be a violation. I think I've got my lesson now. Everyone has to die someday.'

Adam considered Cleopatra's words, realizing the significance of the situation. '"*The secrets of the past enshrined.*" Cleopatra is the one who is enshrined.'

Aunt Mary was listening to Adam, and then she spoke up. 'Cleopatra, what secret are you holding, as the poem suggests?'

Cleopatra fixed her gaze on them, her expression shifting from regret to a glimmer of hope. 'I can only reveal that secret if you free me from this place.'

Emma questioned the practicality of this request. 'But if you are trapped here for eternity, then how do we free you?'

'The shrine's magic binds me here, but there is a way. If someone wishes from the heart for my freedom, the shrine will release me.'

'Hmm... '*hearts ablaze and souls set free, the truth unfolds as you shall see.*' Now, the poem makes sense. When you are freed from the heart, you tell us the secret.' Adam explained.

'But why did Shakespeare not make the wish?'

The answer was wrapped in Shakespeare's own intentions. 'Good question. He said that he may not deserve the secret. Only a great person does. That is why he wrote the poem. He wanted a great person to find this place.'

Empathy for Cleopatra's plight filled their hearts, and Aunt Mary made the heartfelt wish to free the legendary pharaoh from her eternal imprisonment.

'Okay then. Aunt, you make the wish.'

'Wait! It is not so easy.' Cleopatra said.

'Yeah! I know. Nothing is easy.' Emma said with a frustrated tone.

'See that inscription right there?' Cleopatra pointed out an inscription in Morse code.

'Morse? Again?' Emma said.

Aunt Mary started, 'Don't worry, folks, I'm...'

'You'll have to decode it. It is a verse. You will have to say it out loud before you wish.'

Adam spoke up, 'Hmm... '*To a coded verse with a hidden line.*' The inscription is the coded verse, and the wish itself must be the hidden line.'

'Alright! Let me start.' Saying so, Aunt Mary started decoding the Morse code and saying it out loud. '*In the shrine, I kneel and pray for Cleopatra's freedom today. Her power of manipulation, she did misuse, but forgiveness and mercy, I now choose. Grant her a chance to start anew, and may her heart be pure and true.*'

'Great! Now grant the wish,' Cleopatra said.

Without hesitation, she uttered the words, 'I heartily request the shrine to free Cleopatra.'

The very air seemed to ripple with energy as the wish echoed through the chamber. The ground quivered beneath them, and Cleopatra's expression transformed from one of despair to relief. She began to speak, her voice echoing through the stone halls.

'The secret you seek resides within the scroll you hold,' Cleopatra explained, pointing to the cryptic scroll they had taken. 'Its contents are written in the Berber language. Study it well, for it holds the knowledge you desire.'

Then, with a graceful gesture, Cleopatra manipulated space itself. In a breathtaking moment of wonder, they felt as if the world around them had blurred and shifted. When the world came back into focus, they were no longer in the underground shrine but on the sunlit surface. Yes, you read it right. Cleopatra teleported them out of the shrine.

The sands of the Sahara stretched before them, and Cleopatra stood alongside them. With a final smile, she nodded in gratitude. It was a breathtaking revelation.

The past, present, and future were intertwined above the vast desert.

'You better go to the archaeologists and show them that you're alive. They are still trying to discover your tomb.' Adam told Cleopatra.

'Archaeologists?' Cleopatra didn't seem to know who archaeologists were.

'Yeah. They study the past based on ruins, artifacts, and other such things.' Adam explained.

'You study us?' Cleopatra seemed surprised.

'Yeah. I understand what it feels like. If someone from the future comes and tells me, 'Hi, I'm trying to find your tomb.' It will obviously be surprising.'

After Adam said so, Cleopatra bid farewell and teleported.

So, there they were, standing in the blazing Sahara sun, holding a scroll that could rewrite history. I mean, talk about stumbling onto an adventure, right?

Like, I can literally write a poem out of it. Watch this–

Sands, as far as the eye could see,

And in their hands, a ticket to a mystery,

That had puzzled minds for more than a century.

It was like something out of a Hollywood hit, only this time they weren't watching it, but they were living it.

The scroll is ancient and mysterious. They had this cryptic parchment, promising secrets and knowledge untold.

Now, our group of adventurers wasn't your typical group of treasure hunters. They were just regular folks thrown into an extraordinary situation. Aunt Mary, with her vast knowledge, was like a wise old sage.

Emma, wide-eyed and curious, was the enthusiast, always ready to dive headfirst into whatever mystery came their way. And then there was Adam, the thoughtful one, who approached everything with a blend of caution and excitement.

As they unfurled the scroll, its ancient pages crackled, filling the air with a sense of anticipation. It was like opening a portal to the past, one that could potentially change the way we see history. Who wouldn't be excited about that?

But decoding an ancient scroll isn't as easy as it sounds. I mean, it's not like they had Google Translate for ancient languages, right? After all, it was 2003. So, there they were, huddled together, squinting at the faded text, trying to make sense of symbols and words that hadn't been used in centuries.

Aunt Mary, bless her heart, was muttering something about Berber languages and ancient scripts. Emma was wide-eyed, and as usual, her excitement was practically contagious. And Adam, well, he was wearing that expression that said, 'I have no idea what I'm doing, but let's do it anyway.'

There were moments of frustration, sure. I mean, decoding an ancient language isn't exactly a walk in the park. But there were also moments of victory when a symbol made sense or a word clicked into place. Each small victory was like finding a piece of a jigsaw puzzle, slowly revealing the bigger picture.

As they deciphered the scroll, they uncovered a story that was more incredible than they could have ever imagined. It was a tale of lost civilizations, of powerful artifacts, and, of course, of Cleopatra's secret. Who knew that a simple scroll could hold so much knowledge?

They were in the middle of the desert, huddled over a scroll, unraveling secrets that had been buried for centuries. It was a mix of excitement, awe, and a dash of humor because, let's face it, if you can't find humor in decoding ancient mysteries, what can you find it in?

And as they read on, they knew that this was just the beginning. More adventures were waiting for them, more mysteries to solve, and, who knows, maybe a few more laughs along the way. So, dear reader, buckle up because they were just getting started, and who knew what other ancient wonders they would uncover next?

Chapter 11
Visiting an Eye

After their rapid adventure in the Sahara, our friends found themselves holding the ancient scroll that promised to rewrite history.

But as exciting as their discovery was, they still had the matter of getting back to the city. Stuck in the middle of the desert, they faced a peculiar puzzle.

'How do we go back?' Adam asked.

'The button,' Emma reminded Adam.

'What button?'

'Oh, come on! The one that Robert gave us.'

'Who? Robert?'

Aunt Mary, prioritizing meaningful actions over silly conversations, acted decisively. She took out the button and spoke. 'This button, Adam.'

'Oh... The button, which the historian gave us.'

'Yeah. The historian's name was Robert.' Emma sighed.

Yes, it was a comical mix-up of names and a moment of button-related amnesia. Now, with the button in Aunt Mary's hands, they were about to embark on a journey back home. They discovered the uniqueness of time travel and the sometimes forgetful nature of adventurers.

So, with the Sahara's endless expanse still fresh in their minds, Aunt Mary pressed the mysterious button given by Robert. There was a moment of silence, and then a voice crackled through the device.

'Hello, Robert speaking.' The button had a speaker in it!

'Uhm... This is Mary Wilson speaking, and we want to go back to Morocco.'

'Sure. I'll send a copter to... the Algerian Megaliths, right?'

'Yes. How long will it take?' She asked, her curiosity getting the best of her.

Robert's response was almost calm, as if arranging transportation to ancient megaliths was an everyday occurrence. 'Not long.'

They exchanged glances, not entirely sure what 'not long' meant in this context. But they had come this far, and trust in Robert's time-traveling abilities seemed like the best option. After all, they had already met Cleopatra–quite literally.

The three of them waited for around four hours, although Robert said it wouldn't take much time.

They saw a whirlybird coming towards them. It landed, and Robert immediately came out and asked, 'What have you found here in just one day?'

'One day? It seemed like several days to me.' Emma exclaimed.

'It makes sense. Cleopatra said that she was manipulating time inside the shrine to live forever, which means she stopped time.' Adam explained.

'Cleopatra?!' Robert was surprised.

'Yes, Cleopatra. We found Cleopatra. She is not dead. She's alive.'

'Where is she now?'

'She teleported somewhere. I don't know where.'

'That explains why her tomb was never found,' Robert said.

'Okay, so can we talk during the flight?' Aunt Mary suggested.

'Sure,' Robert replied.

The four of them boarded the flight. They took one last look at the vast, awe-inspiring desert around them. The sands stretched endlessly, much like the mysteries they had uncovered.

And while they had Cleopatra's secret tucked away in the ancient scroll, they knew that more adventures awaited them. So, they stood there in the desert, ready to board the copter, the sun's warmth embracing them, their hearts still ablaze with the wonders they had witnessed. Who knew where the next button push would take them and what secrets they'd uncover next? One thing was for sure: They were ready for it, whatever it might be.

'Now tell me. What else did you find?'

'Many things. Firstly, we found a map of the observable universe.'

'Map of the universe? Unbelievable. If you were capable of finding that, then you would be a world-famous archaeologist. Could I see the map?'

'Sure, why not?'

Aunt Mary handed the map of the observable universe to Robert.

'You could sell this to a museum,' Robert suggested.

'Er, I was thinking of giving it to NASA.' Adam said.

'You could do that too. It could tremendously help space research.'

'And then we found this.' Aunt Mary handed Robert the manuscript about elixirs as he returned the map.

'This is probably the greatest discovery ever. I never thought elixirs even existed.'

'I know. If scientists are able to brew these elixirs, then it will change the world.'

Robert thought for a while. 'I don't think that's a good idea. This should rather be kept secret. This should not get into the wrong hands.'

'Then I've got this ancient medical text.' Aunt Mary handed over the text to Robert.

'Herbal remedies... of *Cancer*?!' Robert exclaimed. He was surprised to see that there were cancer remedies during the ancient period.

'Cancer? *Where?*'

'Here. And this is a Berber language. So, you figured out what it was from the pictures, huh?'

'Yes, but how do you know Berber?'

'What do you mean? Berber is one of the local languages of Morocco.'

'So, will you be able to help us with this?' Aunt Mary presented the scroll, which was supposed to be holding some secret.

'What's this?'

'Cleopatra mentioned that it holds a secret. It could also be a clue to the secret. Now, can you translate it for us?'

'Sure.

In Sahara, I quietly lay,
An eye-shaped wonder from an ancient day.
Geological secrets, my layers convey,
What am I, this mysterious display?'

'Great! Another poetry.' Emma was frustrated with the poetry, especially after the Shakespearean one.

'Sahara...eye-shaped wonder...layers... What could it be?' Robert pointed out the critical points of the poem.

'Is there any ruin that looks like an eye?' Adam asked.

'No, there isn't. But I think I know what it is.' Robert replied, digging deeper into the riddle.

'What is it?'

'The Richat Structure. It's also known as the "Eye of The Sahara."'

'And...the layers? How does that relate?'

'So, at first, it was believed that the Richat Structure was an impact site of an asteroid, but now it's believed that it formed through erosion, layer by layer.'

'Then, Eye of the Sahara it is. We'll have to redirect our copter to... Wait, where is it located?'

'Mauritania. It's below Morocco on the map.'

Robert realized that the pilot had no idea of the change of destination. He instructed the pilot to change the destination.

After a few hours, they saw a mystical structure.

'Didn't you say it was geological?' Adam asked.

'Yeah. It formed from erosion. That's what's believed. Nobody knows for sure.'

'That's literally a perfect circle... At least it looks perfect to me.'

In the heart of the desert, an immense circular impression stretched like a massive eye.

The innermost circle of the eye reveals a raised, rocky core that, indeed, looked like a pupil. And then there were all these ridges and troughs around it, like a super intricate pattern.

The bands of sand and rock radiated outwards in these rings that legit looked like the iris of an eye! They were totally mesmerized. It was like a spell or something.

The entire formation seemed to have been sculpted by nature's hand, resembling a massive eye gazing out from the barren expanse of the desert.

'I think there is a reason why it is named 'Eye of Sahara,' Emma said.

'There is a reason for everything, Emma,' Adam replied.

The copter landed on the really, really rocky surface of the desert. (Don't ask how the pilot did that.) The beautiful view from the sky was lost. Now, all they could see was something that looked like rocky dunes merged together.

Adam and Emma stood at the edge of the Eye of the Sahara, the vast circular formation in the middle of the desert. They had come here, guided by the cryptic knowledge they had gained from the underground shrine. The sun beat down on the windswept sands, and the massive geological formation before them was a breathtaking sight.

'What secret will you find here?' Robert asked.

'I know, right? It's just like some rocks arranged in a circle.' Aunt Mary replied.

'There must be something there. Or else, why would the scroll guide us here?' Adam said.

'I'll leave you here, then. And... the button's with you, right?'

'Yes, it's with me,' Aunt Mary said.

Saying so, Robert left in the copter.

'Do you think this looks like it's man-made? It looks so artificial, doesn't it?' Emma asked, still wondering how it could be a natural formation.

'You're right. And that might also be a clue.'

'How?'

'If it is man-made, then there could be something hidden.'

After a while, Aunt Mary spoke from a distance.

'Or maybe the layers have something to tell.'

'What do you mean?' Emma asked. Her curiosity was piqued.

'Yeah, what do you mean by layers? It's just circles of rocks, one inside another.'

'No, these are actual layers. Look.' Aunt Mary pointed at the innermost circle. Inside it were layers of circular rocks, each smaller than the other.

'More perfect circles? It can't be natural. It has to be artificial.' Emma said.

'Robert said that it was once an impact crater, but now it is believed to have formed through geological factors,' Adam said

'Yes, and I think none of them are correct theories.'

'Well, I think the second theory could be partially correct.'

'How?'

'See, till now, all the secrets we found were hidden within chambers.'

'...except the first one,' Emma added.

'Yeah. Now, let me speak. So, if all the secrets we found after the first one were in chambers, then even this secret we're gonna find here must be in a chamber.' Adam said.

'Makes sense, but how does it relate to the second theory?'

'It's simple. Over time, eroded materials must have *covered* up the secret chamber.'

Emma, with her natural curiosity, couldn't help but voice her thoughts. 'So, you are telling me that an already secret chamber was covered up, making it even harder to find? Why can't things be easy?'

Aunt Mary smiled at Emma's comment. 'Everything isn't easy, Emma. Ancient civilizations often went to great lengths to protect their most valuable treasures or their most closely guarded secrets. This chamber might hold something incredibly important or sensitive. That's why it's concealed. Now, let's find the covered-up secret entrance. We might have to crack open rocks to uncover it.' Adam was so calm that I think he's the one who is going to bring about world peace. Like, he's so calm that he even takes a step forward and teaches others to be calm. Well, now it is her sister, but maybe later, it might be the world. Who knows?

'And... how do we crack the rocks?' Emma asked.

'I've got a hammer. Geological hammer, to be precise,' Aunt Mary said.

Adam was fascinated. 'Good thing you've got it, but how did you know we would need it?'

Aunt Mary chuckled. 'Every archaeologist needs one. It's like their trusty sidekick on any adventure. You never know when you'll encounter rocks that need to sacrifice themselves to give up their secrets.'

They walked around the perimeter of the formation, inspecting the various layers. Adam took Aunt Mary's geological hammer and began tapping different sections, listening to the echoes. A deeper sound referred to a hollow section, and a high-pitched sound indicated that there were only air pockets.

After a long journey of knocking, hammering, and tapping (and also making sure no one saw them doing so), Adam spoke up.

'Emma, I think we should focus on areas where the layers seem unusual,' Adam suggested, pointing to a spot where the layers were interrupted by a vertical intrusion of rock. 'These places always seem to be hollow.'

Emma nodded and joined in the investigation. 'Right. If we are able to find any pattern, then we might be able to find the entrance.'

After some time, they identified a section where the layers appeared to separate ever so slightly, forming a hairline crack in the rock.

'It's here, Adam!' Emma exclaimed. 'I think I've found something.'

'The crack. I think it's a result of our tapping. But it also indicates that there is less support for the rock, allowing it to crack.'

'So, is there something below it?'

'Must be.'

Excitement and anticipation filled the air as they carefully examined the crack. They could feel a faint, cool breeze emanating from it. Determined to uncover the secrets hidden within the Eye of the Sahara, they decided to widen the crack to break the rock that they thought was covering their secret. Gently prying, they hoped to trigger a mechanism that might unlock the chamber.

As they worked diligently, the layers of rock began to shift and separate more noticeably. The ground vibrated slightly, and a low rumble filled the air. After a few moments of intense effort, they finally succeeded. The rock finally broke into two massive pieces, revealing an unscathed entrance made of gold.

'It's beautiful. This is gonna be a great tourist attraction.' Emma said.

'Hmph. More like a burglar attraction. Also, let's not forget, Emma, we're the first to open it in centuries. This could be a trove of priceless secrets, and we must approach it with care.' Adam said.

'We just removed the geological layer. What about opening the door itself?'

'We just need to find the lock.'

The three of them inspected the door. Even after a long time, they were not able to find the lock.

In their prior explorations, they encountered a variety of locks, each unique in its design and method of operation. In the Hall of Records, concealed buttons integrated seamlessly into the mosaic-like floor tiles had been their challenge. They had even encountered a lock linked to the periodic table of elements.

Exiting the Hall of Records presented a different puzzle involving the arrangement of levers in a specific sequence. At the entrance to the secret shrine, they had to manipulate dots to align them with the stars above.

This diverse collection of locks emphasized that each challenge was unique in its design and operation. Thus, they couldn't rely on the familiarity of past locks. They had to think outside the box.

Adam's voice bore a hint of despair. 'I've searched every inch of this entrance, and I couldn't find a single trace of a lock. It isn't apparent. It's almost as if the door defies conventional methods of entry.'

The absence of a visible seam on the golden door added to the complexity of their task.

They never thought that a lock or an entrance could be made so complex that it would seem that there wasn't any lock.

Chapter 12
Invisible Entrance

They kept on searching for clues.

Like, how will they even find the secret if they can't even open the door?

Emma thought of their previous adventures. Celestial dance, hieroglyphs, and... wishes 'Wishes!' Emma thought in her mind. Emma had flashbacks from the Valley of Knowledge, where they had to wish for a door for the door to appear. In the secret shrine, they had to wish for a staircase. They also had to wish for Cleopatra to be freed. See? It was like there was something special about wishes in ancient times. It was one thing that they still had not tried on the door they were trying to open right now.

Emma couldn't contain her revelation any longer and blurted out, 'Hey, something just struck my mind.'

Adam, intrigued by her sudden enthusiasm, raised an eyebrow. 'What is it?'

'Remember the pyramid in the Valley of Knowledge?' Emma asked.

Adam nodded, the memory slowly returning. 'Sort of.'

'To enter the pyramid, all we did was wish for a door, and one appeared,' Emma continued.

'Wishes? Again?' Adam questioned, a hint of disbelief in his voice.

Emma pressed on, undeterred, 'Yeah, it's a long shot, but let me try. I wish for a door!' She declared, her voice a blend of hope and doubt.

The three of them waited with bated breath for a moment, but the heavy stone entrance remained stubbornly unyielding. After a collective sigh, Adam conceded, 'Well, it seems wishes don't always work.'

Emma agreed with a hint of disappointment, 'I guess you're right.'

Aunt Mary, who had been quietly observing the failed wishing experiment, decided to involve a bit of practicality in the situation. 'Maybe we're looking in the wrong place,' she calmly suggested.'

'No, we're not, I'm sure,' Adam replied, a touch of determination in his voice.

'Let's continue what we were doing,' Emma suggested.

As Emma and Adam resumed their quest for hidden locks or secret buttons, Aunt Mary decided to examine the scroll. She suspected that it might hold a clue to unlocking this stubborn door. She carefully unfurled the scroll, her brow furrowing in concentration.

Adam, ever the keen observer, noticed something unusual. 'What's that?' he asked, pointing at the backside of the scroll.

'What?' Aunt Mary replied.

'Behind the scroll. There's a mark.' Adam pointed out.

Aunt Mary turned the scroll and discovered a distinctive mark–

⊙

'What is this?' Aunt Mary inquired.

Adam, always ready with a theory, chimed in, 'It looks like some kind of hint, or maybe an ancient doodle from a bored scribe.'

'It's no time for jokes, Adam. Let's be more serious about this,' Aunt Mary said, tired of all the jokes that Adam and Emma crack.

Emma, who was still occupied in her search for a hidden lock, had yet to notice the mysterious mark behind the scroll.

'Emma, come here,' Adam called out.

Aunt Mary pointed at the mark. 'What do you think this is?'

Emma walked over. 'A mark… perhaps it's a hint related to the lock. How did we miss checking the back of the scroll before?' She observed it carefully.

'What do you think the circle means?' Aunt Mary asked.

Adam observed the mark. 'I think it refers to the door itself. The door does seem to be a perfect circle.'

'Then, what about the dot in the middle?' Emma asked.

'*That* might be the real clue,' Adam said.

'What? You mean the lock is in the middle of the door?' Emma asked.

'Must be.'

'But we checked the whole door. There was no lock.'

'It could be hidden.'

With renewed determination, Adam walked to the middle of the door, and Aunt Mary and Emma followed. In the center of the door, they found only a shallowly carved circle, a part of the intricate design that decorated the golden surface. The lock was supposed to be right in front of them, and they were ready to unlock the secrets concealed behind the circular gateway.

'How is that the lock?' Emma asked, her brow furrowed in confusion.

Adam shook his head. 'No idea.'

'And if that is the lock, then where is the key?' Emma continued.

'Again, no idea,' Adam replied, his frustration rising as they both inspected the shallowly carved circle.

They pushed it, turned it, and even tried hammering it with Aunt Mary's geological hammer, but nothing happened.

'I think I know how this works,' Adam said suddenly, his eyes lighting up with realization after investigating the lock for a while.

'How?' Emma asked.

'I think this isn't just a decorative carving. It's a socket. We'll need to put something in, something that fits like a key,' Adam explained his theory.

'I was thinking the same, but what could be the key? If we don't find it, we can't get in,' Emma said. Her frustration seemed to be more than Adam's.

Adam fell into deep thought. As he stared at the scroll, something about it seemed out of place. He turned to Emma with a sudden realization.

'Do you see the scroll rod?' Adam asked Emma.

'Yeah,' Emma replied, puzzled.

'Do you think scroll rods normally look like that?' Adam continued.

'Hmm... I don't think so,' Emma replied, realizing what Adam was getting at.

What seemed odd about the scroll was the scroll rod itself. Typically, the ends of scroll rods were bulb-shaped for easier handling, but the one they had was different—it had flat ends.

Emma stared at the scroll rod, her mind racing with possibilities. Then it struck her.

Emma examined the scroll. 'Now I see. The rod's ends look flat. That's unusual.'

Adam nodded, a glorious smile forming on his face. 'Exactly. The scroll rod itself is the key.'

'Huh?' Emma said, confusion giving way to curiosity.

Without hesitation, Adam implanted the flat end of the scroll rod into the circular socket on the door. A low, rumbling sound echoed through their surroundings, and the ground beneath their feet trembled.

'The door's opening!' Adam shouted. His voice was barely audible over the rumble.

Slowly, with a deep, grinding noise, the massive door began to shift. A feeling of expectancy and nervousness filled the air as the ancient gateway, sealed for centuries, creaked open, revealing the mysteries that lay beyond.

In the middle of the Eye of Sahara, the door opened, leaving the three with a choice.

'Should we jump in?' Emma asked.

'Drop something,' Adam suggested.

'What can we drop?'

'The scroll, maybe. I don't think it will be of use anymore.' Adam replied.

'But if we remove it from the socket, the door might close,' Emma said.

'Well, that could happen... Then what do we do?'

'Jump in?'

'No. Too risky.'

'Hmm... Wait... We forgot something.'

'What?'

'We are surrounded by rocks!'

'Oh! Right. I totally forgot.'

'I'll get a rock.'

Saying so, Emma picked up a hefty rock.

'Argh... Too heavy.'

'Get a lighter one!' Adam yelled.

Emma got a rock and handed it over to Adam.

'Ready?'

'Yes'

Adam dropped the rock into what looked like an endless void. This time, the rock reached the floor quicker.

'Okay then. We're cleared to jump.' Emma said.

'I'll jump first.' Saying this, Adam jumped in. 'It's a safe fall!' he yelled from inside.

'Okay then. I'm jumping in.' Emma jumped in, too.

Aunt Mary didn't want to jump in.

'You guys move on. I just don't want to jump. I have a fear of heights.' Aunt Mary said.

'Okay then. We'll have to move on without her.' Emma said.

'Yeah. I never knew she was afraid of heights.'

After walking for a while, they found a passageway in the dim light.

They started walking towards the passageway that was in sight. After a while, they entered the passageway. After a few minutes, they encountered a door.

'A door. Do you think we should open it?' Emma asked.

'Obviously, yes. Why are you asking?'

Adam pushed open the door. The light inside was revealed. They were met with a sight that left them awestruck. The chamber was not only spacious but also intricately adorned with carvings, symbols, and artifacts that seemed to belong to a civilization lost in time.

'This reminds me of the Hall of Records. The time we pushed open the door.' Emma said.

'Yeah. But this is different. This looks like a palace.'

'This place is incredible! Why did you call it a palace, though?

'Take a look around, Emma. It's like a treasure trove in here! These artifacts, the intricately designed jewelry, the ornate statues, and the beautifully crafted pottery all scream 'luxury.' That's why I called it a palace.'

'I see what you mean. These pieces are stunning. Just look at the details on this jewelry and the craftsmanship on these statues. I can't believe these artifacts have been hidden away for so long. It's like discovering a lost chapter of history.'

'That's the beauty of archaeology, Emma. Uncovering these hidden gems that offer us a glimpse into the past.'

Stacked neatly on shelves were countless scrolls and manuscripts, their ancient pages filled with written knowledge. These texts covered a wide range of subjects, including astronomy, mathematics, medicine, and philosophy.

Emma saw them and was like, 'Adam, look at all these scrolls and manuscripts!'

And then Adam noticed that something was written on the floor they were walking on.

'Hey, Emma, check this out. Look at the floor. There's a gigantic celestial map etched into it!' Adam said, pointing to the floor.

'Wow, that's amazing! I can see stars, constellations, and all sorts of celestial stuff. It's just like the one we found at the shrine.'

'Right? I think this map is the key to how this civilization understood the universe. It also tells us that not only the Zingh Empire was knowledgeable about the universe.

'It's mind-blowing to think about how advanced they must have been.'

'Absolutely, Emma. It's like they were masters of the universe or something. This place just keeps getting more fascinating.'

As they explored further, they discovered a hidden hall within the chamber.

Its walls were adorned with paintings depicting celestial phenomena, the alignment of stars, and the movements of planets. In the center of this hall stood a giant, ornate sundial that indicated specific dates and times of celestial significance.

As they reached the end of this celestial corridor, Adam couldn't contain his excitement. 'Emma, come check this out! There's something written on that wall.'

Emma, always up for a bit of linguistic detective work, leaned in. 'What does it say, Adam?'

'I don't know. It's in some weird language.'

Emma looked at the inscription and observed it carefully.

Emma looked at the inscription and observed it carefully. 'I think I've seen this language before.'

'What do you think it is?'

'Hmm... It's the same language that was on the scroll.'

'You mean Berber language?'

'Yeah.'

Adam, ever the diligent note-taker, grabbed his notebook and diligently copied down the inscription. 'I'll ask Robert to translate it.'

It was clear that they had stumbled upon an extraordinary treasure trove of ancient knowledge and wisdom, one that could reshape our understanding of history and science.

But the question remained. What would they do with this newfound place, and how would it impact the world above?

'Okay. Now that we've got the inscription and that this is the end of the passageway, how do we get out of it?' Emma asked.

The question echoed in Adam's mind. They'd made it in, but finding the exit was like solving an ancient riddle in itself.

'One solution is to go back to the entrance. Aunt Mary is outside so that she could get a rope or something.' Adam said.

Emma raised an eyebrow, not thrilled by the prospect. 'Or... we could find the exit. I don't wanna go all the way back to the entrance.'

'You're right. The return trip sounds like an epic quest of its own. Let's hunt for an exit right here.' Adam agreed with Emma's point.

'Great plan. Maybe there's a hidden door somewhere.'

'Let's search, then,' Adam said.

Saying this, they start inspecting. The two of them began a thorough search of the chamber's walls, inspecting for hidden doors, buttons, or any signs that might indicate an exit.

They ran their hands over the stone surfaces, tapped, pushed, and even tried a bit of wall-wrestling, but alas, the wall revealed no secrets.

After a while of fruitless searching, Adam spoke up. 'I can't find anything. Is this place like a one-way ticket to the center of the Earth or something?'

As time passed, they grew more frustrated and tired. Adam sighed, sitting down to rest against one of the walls.

'Ugh! Going all the way back now feels like the ultimate anticlimax.' Emma leaned against the opposite wall, feeling drained out. As she leaned, the section of the wall she pressed against shifted slightly, like a button being depressed.

A soft, rumbling sound filled the chamber.

'Did you hear that?' Emma asked, her eyes widening.

Then, slowly, a previously concealed doorway swung open before them.

'Whoa, Emma, you did it! You found the exit!

'I did? I mean, yeah, I totally meant to do that.'

They didn't waste time talking about it and rushed toward the newfound passage. It revealed a stone staircase leading upward. The siblings exchanged excited glances before ascending the stairs, and as they exited, they found themselves at the edge of the Eye of Sahara.

'Wow, that was some crazy adventure, huh?'

'Absolutely! And look at this view. We made it out, and now we're standing at the edge of the Eye of Sahara.'

'I guess sometimes you just need to push the right buttons—or walls, in this case.'

'Haha, right. Now, we should head back and tell Aunt Mary about all the incredible things we found.'

With that, they left behind the mysteries of the underground shrine, stepping into the brilliant Saharan sunlight, eager to share their tales of adventure with Aunt Mary.

Chapter 13
The Prophecy

They walked back to where Aunt Mary was waiting and began recounting the story of their underground journey.

'How was your journey?'

'Aunt Mary, you won't believe what we've seen! It was like a hidden palace filled with the most amazing treasures and knowledge.' Emma was very excited to see Aunt Mary. To her, a few minutes without her felt like they had been apart for years.

'A palace? You guys certainly had quite the adventure.'

'And the scrolls! They were filled with knowledge about astronomy, mathematics, medicine, and philosophy. There were even maps of the universe on the floor that left us speechless.'

'Sounds incredible! What else did you find?'

'We also discovered inscriptions in the Berber language, and there was a massive sundial in a hidden hall. It's like this civilization had a profound understanding of the cosmos.'

'Oh, and about the inscription, as it was in Berber, we weren't able to read it. But Robert can read it for us.'

'That's remarkable! You've found something truly extraordinary.'

'It was like an archaeological dream come true.'

'I'm so proud of both of you for your hard work and determination. This discovery could change everything we know about history and science.'

'Yeah, and now we're faced with a new problem. What do we do with this place? As Adam had already told, it would be a great burglar attraction.'

'That's a responsibility we'll have to consider carefully. But for now, let's celebrate this incredible discovery. Who knows what other mysteries lie hidden beneath the sands of the Sahara?'

As they stood on the edge of the Eye of Sahara, the siblings, along with Aunt Mary, exchanged knowing glances. The weight of their incredible journey had profoundly impacted them, and it was time to return to the world above.

Emma nudged Aunt Mary, her voice tinged with urgency, 'Press the button.'

Aunt Mary looked puzzled for a moment, and then it clicked. 'Robert's button, right?'

'*Exactly*! We need to get out of here,' Emma emphasized.

Aunt Mary pressed the button, and soon enough, they heard Robert's voice on the other end.

'Hello. Robert speaking.'

Aunt Mary quickly identified herself, 'This is Mary Wilson, and we need you to pick us up.'

Robert, ever the efficient one, replied, 'Sure. I'll be there in an hour.'

The three of them exchanged doubtful glances.

'I doubt he'll actually be here in an hour,' Aunt Mary muttered.

Emma chimed in, 'Yeah, remember last time he said 'Not long,' and we ended up waiting for four hours.'

Adam chuckled, 'So, our best bet is that he'll be fashionably late once again. We know the drill.'

Turns out, their estimation was pretty spot on. Robert did arrive after three hours this time, and everyone agreed it was a significant improvement.

As they spotted the copter in the distance, Aunt Mary couldn't resist a small victory, 'Told you he was going to take more than an hour.'

Adam nodded, 'Yeah, but let's give credit where it's due. Robert's been a great help. Without him, we wouldn't even be here.'

Robert deboarded the copter.

'Hi, guys! What did...' Robert was speechless when he saw the gold door. 'Is that a gold door?'

Proudly, Adam confirmed, 'Yes, we found it there.'

Robert's eyes widened in amazement. 'How did you discover it?'

Emma grinned, 'We just broke the rock that was covering it, easy-peasy.'

Robert was thoroughly impressed, 'Wow!'

But the question remained. What secrets had they discovered in the underground chamber? Robert was eager to hear the details.

Aunt Mary suggested they continue the conversation during their flight. 'Can we talk after we board the copter?'

'Sure, hop in,' Robert replied, leading them back to the aircraft, where they could share their extraordinary findings in comfort.

Back in the copter, the group found their seats, and a sense of keenness filled the air. Robert couldn't contain his curiosity any longer.

'So, what did you find down there? That gold door alone must be a remarkable discovery,' Robert inquired, still somewhat fixated on the door.

Adam began recounting the adventure with enthusiasm, 'Oh, Robert, you won't believe what's inside that chamber! It's like a treasure trove of ancient knowledge and history. We found incredible artifacts, intricately designed jewelry, ornate statues, and beautifully crafted pottery. It's like stepping into the past.'

'Those are incredible artifacts. If we are able to find out which civilization these belonged to, we might be able to know a lot more about them.'

Emma chimed in, excitement dancing in her eyes, 'And those scrolls and manuscripts, Robert! Countless of them, all filled with written knowledge. We're talking about astronomy, mathematics, medicine, and philosophy. It's like the ancient library of Alexandria down there.'

'Woah! I've never seen such a massive number of discoveries made in one day. I'll notify all my colleagues to investigate them.'

Adam leaned forward, eager to share his favorite part, 'And the floor, Robert, it's etched with a massive map of the universe. It's detailed, showing stars, constellations, and celestial events. We believe this map holds the key to how they manipulated celestial occurrences.'

'Yeah. It was just like the one we found at the shrine, but the one we found today seemed to have more information.'

Robert was almost at a loss for words, 'That's... simply astounding. This is like a dream come true for archaeologists. It's gonna rewrite the books on history, isn't it?'

Aunt Mary nodded, 'Indeed, it will. But there's more. We found inscriptions and writings in the Berber language.'

Robert leaned back in his seat, digesting the magnitude of their discovery. 'This is a turning point, not just for you but for the world. We'll need to proceed with caution, sharing this knowledge wisely so it benefits all of humanity.'

As the copter soared above the Sahara, the group continued their discussion, anticipating the profound consequences of their adventure. The world was about to change, and their lives were forever intertwined with the secrets of the Eye of the Sahara.

'And, coming back to the inscription, we did not understand what was written, so I copied it down in my notebook. I want you to translate it.' Adam handed over his notebook to Robert.

After reading the script, Robert spoke. 'Hmm. This is a prophecy from the past.'

'That's fascinating. Can you read the whole prophecy?'

'Sure.

In the distant future, curious minds and open hearts shall find the secrets of our long-lost realm. They find our allies of Gedi, unite the wisdom of the past with the present, forging a brighter future.'

'I think this prophecy was meant for us,' Emma said.

'I think everything in the first person refers to the people who built the Eye of Sahara, and everything in the third person refers to us,' Adam said.

'I think you're right,' Emma said.

'We found the secrets of the long-lost realm. Then, next, we have to find... Gedi?'

'What's that?'

'Gedi ruins. It's situated in Kenya. A long journey from here,' Robert said.

'We're going there then.'

As they discussed the intriguing prophecy, the atmosphere in the copter buzzed with excitement.

Robert read it carefully and said, 'I can't believe it. It's like a message meant just for you.'

Adam shared a smile with Emma, 'Yeah, it's almost like the people who built this place knew we would come along someday. It's a bit strange.'

As the copter continued its journey, the group delved into deciphering the prophecy they had found. Robert, still intrigued, shared his thoughts, 'You know, this prophecy could be more than just a message; it could be a guide for our journey.'

Emma nodded, 'Absolutely! It's like the ancient civilization anticipated that someone would come along to rediscover their legacy. It's as if they're passing the torch of knowledge to us.'

Adam chimed in, 'And we're the ones to explore the ruins of Gedi, their allies. It's like they left a breadcrumb trail for us to follow.'

Robert smiled, 'You're right. This adventure keeps getting more exciting. But it's not gonna be a short journey. Gedi is in Kenya, quite a distance from here.'

Aunt Mary chuckled, 'Well, we might be in the pilot's bad books for frequently changing our destination.'

Emma grinned, 'I guess he should get used to our spontaneous decisions by now.'

Adam nodded in agreement, 'Yep, changing destinations is becoming our characteristic. But the adventure is worth it!'

After informing the pilot about their change of plans, the group leaned back in their seats, eagerness building as they headed toward their next destination, Gedi.

The pilot sighed and rolled his eyes as he adjusted their flight path to head toward the Gedi ruins in Kenya.

After several hours of travel, they reached the Gedi ruins. It was near a forest. It covered a vast area.

As the group arrived at the Gedi ruins in Kenya, they were met with a sense of awe. The ancient stone structures, overgrown with vines and surrounded by lush greenery, spoke volumes about the civilization that once thrived there.

'Guys, can I join you this time? I think I've been missing out on the amazing adventures.' Robert asked. He really felt unhappy about missing out on the exciting adventures.

'Sure! You could be a great help to us.' Emma said.

Excited to begin their search, Adam suggested, 'Let's split up and explore different areas. Maybe we'll find something interesting.'

Adam's attention went towards a series of ruined stone structures, carefully examining the architectural remnants.

He took notes on his findings, attempting to piece together the layout and purpose of the ancient buildings.

Aunt Mary was exploring a shaded corner of the ruins, where she had uncovered a collection of pottery shards.

Adam, who was occupied with studying the stone structures, called out to the others.

'Hey, guys, these structures are fascinating! I'm pretty sure they had some specific purpose. Maybe dwellings, or perhaps something else entirely!'

'Archaeologists have already explored that. It is named The House of the Dhow,' Robert told Adam.

Aunt Mary, her hands filled with pottery shards, responded, 'You won't believe the pottery I've found over here! It's incredible how well-preserved some of these pieces are. I wish we had an expert with us to date them accurately.'

'An expert, huh?' Robert said.

'Yeah.'

'I think you forgot that you have an expert right here.'

'Oh! Right. Then tell me something useful about these shards.'

'Hmm... Not much to decipher.'

'How old do you think this is?'

'Not old. Probably a few years old. If it were from the lost civilization, then it would already have reached the museum.' Robert said.

Aunt Mary was disappointed with what Robert said. She thought that the pottery shards would have something interesting to say.

Robert went near the entrance, inspecting the carvings and inscriptions on a massive stone gate.

His keen eyes observed the intricate symbols, trying to decipher any meaning they might hold in the context of the ancient civilization that once thrived here.

'What do you think the gate was an entrance to?' Adam asked.

'In ancient times, intricate carvings meant luxury. I guess this was an entrance to the dwelling of the royal family of the civilization.'

'You mean the palace?' Adam asked with curiosity.

'Yeah. Something like that.' Robert replied.

Robert, still examining the massive stone gate, chimed in, 'These carvings are like nothing I've ever seen. I'll need to take detailed rubbings and try to decipher their meaning. It's like solving a giant puzzle.'

Meanwhile, Emma, who was always curious, ventured towards a crumbling wall near the center of the ruins.

Carefully inspecting the stones, her fingers traced the patterns etched into the ancient bricks. Suddenly, she felt a loose stone. With a gentle push, it shifted, revealing a hidden compartment.

'Hey guys, I think I found something here!' Emma called out.

'What is it, Emma?' Adam asked.

'Looks like our little explorer has stumbled upon a discovery.' Aunt Mary said.

'It's a hidden compartment!' Emma said.

'Now, how did you find it?' Robert asked.

'There was a loose stone here, so I pushed it in.'

'Well, it's true that sometimes you need to push the right... stones.' Adam said, recalling the time when Emma pushed a section of the wall, revealing an exit.

Excitedly, they gathered around her. Inside the compartment, they discovered a series of scrolls and parchments.

'What are these about?' Adam asked.

Robert picked one up and said, 'These seem to be records of the Gedi administration. It mentions their leaders, trade routes, and even their alliances with neighboring civilizations.'

Adam added, 'This compartment has a lot of historical information. Let's collect these and decipher them later. Who knows what secrets they might reveal?'

'Right. It's gonna help us to know a lot more about our past.' Robert said.

Adam looked at the scrolls. He noticed something. The scrolls were in English. 'Robert, these scrolls are in English.'

'Yeah. I noticed that.'

'But I thought they would be in the language of Gedi or something.'

'You are in Kenya, Adam. You'll find many English speakers here. The English language of the scrolls tells us that they are not too old. They are probably from the time when Kenya was under British colonial rule.' Robert explained.

'British colonial rule. That explains it.' Adam understood.

Adam was still into the scrolls. He carefully read each and every scroll.

One of them, as Robert said, contained information about the administration. Another scroll had information about every single person in the royal family. Some of them included autobiographies of the rulers.

Adam kept on checking through the scrolls. None of them had information that would help their quest. After a while, one scroll caught Adam's attention.

'Guys! I found something.'

'What did you find?' Robert asked

'It's another poem.'

This was the poetry:

Within the royal house, you tread with care,
Seek< the hidden button, don't> let it ensnare.
In the dhow, the bowl, and the west wall's grace,
Repeat the hidden act in this ancient place.
As you unveil the clue to your next visit's plot,
The secrets of your journey will never be forgotten.

'It looks like a clue to me,' Robert said.

'It is a clue, but what does it mean?' Adam asked.

Robert reread the poem. 'Within the royal house, we seek a button.'

'And… we don't let it ensnare?' Adam was confused.

'Ensnare means tangle. So…'

'…That means that we have to press the button, but the button can tangle us. Right?'

'I think so.'

Adam noticed that Emma and Aunt Mary were still busy with their work. 'Emma, aunt! Come here!'

'What is it?' Emma asked.

'It's a poem, and we need to find a button in the royal house. We just have to find it. Don't press it.'

'Okay.' Emma and Aunt Mary went to what Robert referred to as the royal house.

Emma, with her keen eyes, was able to find a loose stone. Two, to be precise.

'Adam! I found two loose stones, and I did not press them as you instructed.'

'Great!'

Robert came and said, 'Don't let it ensnare. One is a trap. We have to choose the right one.'

'How do we know which button isn't trapped?' Emma asked.

Aunt Mary chimed in, 'I found something odd.'

'What is it?' Adam asked.

‘This line,’ Aunt Mary said, pointing to the line-

Seek‹ the hidden button, don’t› let it ensnare.

'Hmm, now I see it. You're referring to the arrows, right?’

‘Yes, and I think it is supposed to be read like this: *Seek left; don’t right.*’

‘So, we press the left one and not the right button.’

Emma heard it and pressed the left button. Nothing happened.

‘Nothing happened. Why?’

‘Because we did not complete the poem, Emma,’ Adam said.

‘Oh!’

Robert reread the poem. ‘*In the dhow, the bowl, and the west wall’s grace, Repeat the hidden act in this ancient place.* I know what it means.’

‘What?’ Adam asked.

‘“*Dhow*” refers to the House of the Dhow. The one you were investigating. “*Bowl*” must refer to the House of the Porcelain Bowl and “*West Wall.*"'

‘...is the House of the West Wall. I get it.’ Emma continued.

‘We have to “*repeat the hidden act*,” which is pressing the left button,’ Adam said.

‘Yes.’

Emma, as always, found the hidden buttons in all three places.

'This is the last button to press.' Emma pressed the last button, and the floor below them opened up.

'Another chamber! Are we in a world full of hidden chambers or something?' Adam was fed up with hidden chambers.

'I guess so,' Emma said.

Chapter 14
The Chamber of Whispers

Lucky for our courageous explorers, the hidden chamber welcomed them with a grand staircase.

Emma's eyes sparkled with delight as she exclaimed, 'Stairs! My favorite thing after ice cream!' Yes, and if you have read the previous chapters, then you must know that till now, this was the first time they have ever encountered a staircase waiting for them at the entrance of a secret chamber.

'Lucky us.' As Adam said so, the group of four ventured into the chamber and descended the staircase.

The four of them stepped onto the staircase. They start ascending down the staircase. Emma, the one who is always curious, took her attention towards the walls of the staircase. Nah, no more hieroglyphs or carvings. This time, it was something totally different.

'Guys! Look at the walls!'

'What about it?' Adam asked.

'The stone. It is... glowing!'

The others noticed it, too. The stone was glowing in the dark, making the walls luminous.

'It's like the walls are made of lights,' Emma added.

'It's nothing surprising to me,' Robert said.

'Why? Rocks can't glow, can they?'

'It's a natural thing. Some rocks got that nightlight talent, you know.' Robert replied.

'Wow! I'm learning new things.'

'Yeah. I'm learning more than what I learn at school!' Adam said.

'Seriously, you all and your rock talk are irritating me. Can we move on? We're not here to admire walls,' Aunt Mary said.

'I know we aren't here to admire walls, but this wall... I just couldn't resist admiring it.' Emma said.

And off they went, exploring mysteries while enjoying their indeed *illuminating* adventure.

The newly discovered chamber was shrouded in an eerie silence, broken only by their hushed breaths and the sound of their footsteps echoing off the ancient stone walls. As they cautiously went further into the depths of the chamber, they were met with an astonishing sight.

The room was beautified with ancient carvings that were hardly readable. They depicted mythical creatures and elaborate rituals. The ceiling was adorned with constellations. Most importantly, in the center of the chamber, there was a mysterious pedestal with a crystal orb glowing softly, casting an indistinct light across the chamber.

'What's that?' Emma asked as she noticed the orb.

'It's an orb. Can't you see?' Adam replied.

'I know it's an orb. I want to know the purpose of the orb being here.'

Aunt Mary inspected the orb and said, 'This must be important. Perhaps it's a source of power for this hidden chamber.'

Emma approached the crystal orb. As she reached out to touch it, her fingers tingled with a strange energy. 'It feels... alive, like it's connected to something vast and ancient.'

Aunt Mary, her scientific mind engaged, observed, 'It's fascinating how ancient civilizations often encoded their knowledge. This crystal might be the key to deciphering our next move.'

'You're right. Everywhere we went, we found ancient knowledge and secrets that were contained within places hidden from the world that we know.'

Adam, meanwhile, was drawn to the carvings on the walls. They seemed to tell a story. A story that held the key to unraveling the mysteries of this chamber.

'Look at these carvings. They seem to depict a series of events–rituals, maybe–involving the crystal orb.' Adam spoke.

Robert, being a historian, said, 'Let me see.'

Saying so, Robert began translating the inscriptions that accompanied the carvings.

'These inscriptions mention a powerful orb known as the Whispering Crystal. It's said to hold the wisdom of the ancient civilization that built this place.'

'Yeah. Orb. It's right in front of us.' Emma said.

'Forget that. What we need is the ancient wisdom of this place.' Adam said.

'But how do we unlock this wisdom?' Emma wondered aloud.

'I believe the poem we deciphered earlier holds the key,' Aunt Mary said, her eyes fixed on the crystal orb.

'You're right. We've followed its clues this far. There must be more to it.' Emma said.

Adam, feeling determined to unveil the secrets that the orb held, reread the poem.

'In the royal house, you tread with care,
Seek the hidden button, don't let it ensnare.

In the dhow, the bowl and the west wall's grace
Repeat the hidden act in this ancient place.
As you unveil the clue to your next visit's plot,
The secrets of your journey will never be forgot.'

As he finished speaking, a low hum filled the chamber, and the crystal orb began to glow brighter, illuminating the carvings in a mesmerizing display.

'It's glowing brighter!' Emma exclaimed. Her eyes filled with awe.

The carvings seemed to come to life, depicting a series of rituals and ceremonies being performed with the Whispering Crystal at the center. It showed the ancient people communicating with heavenly beings, harnessing the power of the stars, and channeling their knowledge into the crystal.

'That must be the ancient knowledge,' Robert said. 'I'll note down what I see. Adam, could you give me your notebook and a pen?'

'Sure.' Adam handed over his notebook and a pen to Robert.

'And, coming back to the orb,' Adam started, 'I think that this orb holds the knowledge that we need to... Wait. Why are we even here again?'

'Argh... You forgot the main purpose of the quest? We came here to know why our parents disappeared.'

'Oh... right. So, this orb must be holding the knowledge that we need to continue our quest to find the reason for our parents' disappearance.' Adam continued.

Robert chimed in. '"*As you unveil the clue to your next visit's plot,*" so, according to the poem, we will unveil the clue to our next visit's plot.'

'But how do we unveil the clue?' Adam said. His mind was in deep connection with the orb.

Aunt Mary stepped forward. Her gaze was fixed on the crystal orb, too. 'I think that we all need to do what Adam did.'

'What did he do?' Emma asked.

'He read the whole poem. Remember how the orb glowed brighter when he did that?'

'Right. The poem *must* be the key.' Emma agreed.

Saying this, the four of them read the whole poem together. After they finished reading it, the orb flashed brightly.

A surge of energy enveloped them, and the room seemed to come alive with whispers of forgotten knowledge.

Visions flashed before their eyes—of distant galaxies, ancient civilizations, and the secrets of the universe. They were traveling into the wisdom of a civilization lost to time.

'Wow! Look at these,' Emma said.

'Yeah. It's beautiful. The night sky is so clear. Every single star and galaxy are visible.' Adam said.

'I wish that nowadays we had a similar night sky.'

'I'll note them down. They could help us later.' Robert said.

Then, suddenly, the vision changed. They saw a vast expanse of white sand stretching to the horizon, the sun casting long shadows on the dunes.

'Whoa, this must be our next destination,' Adam exclaimed, his eyes wide with amazement.

Emma nodded in agreement, her voice filled with excitement, 'It's incredible! I've never seen anything like it. What is it?'

'It's the White Desert,' Robert replied.

'Wow! I never thought that a desert could be white!'

'But where is it located?' Adam said.

'All the way back in Egypt,' Robert replied.

As the visions subsided, they found themselves standing in the chamber, their minds brimming with newfound understanding.

'We did it!' Emma breathed. Her voice was filled with joy.

'We've unlocked the secrets of the Whispering Crystal,' Adam said, his eyes shining with excitement.

Excitement filled the air as they decided to unravel this new mystery.

'To Egypt, then?' Aunt Mary suggested, her eyes shining with expectation.

'Absolutely! Let's follow this trail and see where it leads us.' Adam exclaimed. His enthusiasm was clearly visible.

As the group prepared to leave the Whispering Crystal Chamber, their minds buzzed with anticipation for their next adventure. They made their way back up the glowing stone staircase, the whispers of the crystal's ancient secrets echoing in their thoughts.

Aunt Mary, ever the realist, pointed out, 'We need to prepare ourselves. The desert can be unforgiving, and we can't afford to underestimate its challenges.'

'Come on! Let's board the chopper!' Robert said. He was eager to go to the White Desert.

'Yeah! What are we waiting for?' Adam said as they boarded the copter.

With renewed determination, they left the Gedi ruins as the copter took off. They were carrying brand-new knowledge and a thrilling lead that would take them on yet another adventure, this time to the White Desert in Egypt.

Hours passed as they finally reached the sands of the White Desert. They marveled at the strange landscape, navigating through towering dunes and natural rock formations.

'It's beautiful,' Emma said.

'Yeah. Nature has carved such beautiful sculptures.' Adam said.

'Those are called mushroom rocks. And... the rocks are limestone,' Robert mentioned.

'Isn't limestone... chalk?' Adam asked.

'Yeah. You could say so. The formations are brittle, so they are highly guarded.' Robert added on.

The copter slowly landed on the desert's surface.

As they prepared for their journey to the White Desert in Egypt, Aunt Mary noticed a stack of parchments in Adam's bag.

'Adam, why do you have a stack of parchments in your bag?' She inquired, her eyes fixed on the ancient-looking papers.

Adam, momentarily surprised, looked at the parchments and then back at Aunt Mary. 'I... don't know.'

'Let me see,' Emma said, looking at the parchments. 'Oh, those? Those are from the Hall of Records.'

'Hall of Records?' Adam asked.

'Yeah. Remember the Labyrinth of Records?'

'Labyrinth? You all went through a labyrinth?' Robert asked.

'That was last year, right?' Adam grinned.

'Argh, logically, yes.'

'Oh.... Now I remember. While going through the labyrinth, we found a few parchments, and I picked them up for decoding them later on.' Adam said.

'And also, the stack of parchments we found on a table. I told you to take them.' Aunt Mary realized.

Robert said, 'Let's take a look at them. They might hold clues that are relevant to our quest.'

'Yeah. We never decoded them, although we thought about decoding them later on.' Adam said.

The group gathered around as the parchments were stacked out in front of them.

'That's... A huge stack,' Rober exclaimed.

'We can't decode all this in one day. It's gonna take quite a lot of time.' Adam said as he wondered how they were going to decode the hundreds of parchments.

'We need to find out the ones that have something written on them. I remember that not all have text on it.' Emma suggested.

As per her words, they began to inspect the stack thoroughly. It turned out that her words were indeed correct. Not every item in the stack contained a message that needed to be decoded.

But, as they went through the stack, they thought that none of them had any text.

'Are you sure that any of them have any text? It seems like all are empty.' Robert asked with doubt.

'Let's just keep searching,' Emma said with confidence.

Indeed, after a while, Robert found a parchment.

'These appear to be clues, possibly related to our search in the White Desert,' Robert said, his brow furrowed in concentration. 'But they're in poetic form, much like the poem that led us here.'

Emma leaned in. Her curiosity amplified. 'What do they say? Are they about the White Desert?'

Robert nodded.

This is the poem that was written on the parchment:

In the land of ivory sands,
Where time stands still,
Where the sun-lit dunes,
Conceal secrets until,

Five limestone guardians,

In their silent grace,

Hold pieces of the truth,

In this ancient place.

The group exchanged puzzled glances. 'Limestone guardians?' Adam questioned.

'Robert, didn't you say that these rock formations are made of limestone?' Adam asked.

'Yes,'

'...and they are heavily guarded.'

'Also, yes.' Robert saw where Adam was going.

'What if the guards are the guardians? They are the guardians of the limestone, right?'

'That doesn't make sense at all,' Emma said.

Aunt Mary, always the logical one, looked around and pointed to five distinct limestone rock formations in the distance. 'I think we may have found our guardians.'

'What?'

'Those rock formations themselves.'

'Let's go check them out,' Adam suggested.

Chapter 15
Limestone Adventure

With a new goal of searching Five different limestone formations that were referred to as limestone guardians, they were eager to discover the secrets that they were destined to find.

At the first limestone formation, they carefully searched for clues. And to their amazement, they found pieces of aged paper hidden within a crevice.

'Hey, folks! I struck gold... well, paper gold, kind of!' Emma called upon the rest of her group.

'Well then, show me this gold of yours,' Adam asked, curious to know how his sister found the piece of paper, which she referred to as gold... or paper gold. Well, a clue is gold, right? Especially when it might lead them to the truth behind their parents' disappearance. Next time someone brags that they have gold, tell them that you have paper.

'Right in the crack!' Emma giggled. 'This paper must be holding the recipe for the best pyramids!'

'I don't think it's related to pyramids!' Adam laughed. 'Let's see what secret it holds.'

As they unfolded the piece of paper, this is what they saw:

Beneath the limes

secre

Underneath the

'What is this?' Adam was confused.

'I don't know. It seems incomplete to me.'

'I think I know why it is incomplete.' Aunt Mary said.

'Then why don't you tell us?'

'So, the poem said, 'Five limestone guardians, In their silent grace, Hold pieces of truth'.'

'So... This is one of the five pieces of truth.'

'Yeah. We must find four more.'

Saying so, they went to search the next limestone guardian for another piece.

This time, Adam was the one to find the text... But there was a problem.

'Guys! I think I found the next piece,' Adam called upon the rest.

'Great!' Robert said.

'But... where is the piece of paper?' Emma asked as she expected Adam to be holding the piece of paper, but he didn't.

'It's up there. I can't reach it.' Adam said, pointing at a crevice high up in the rock.'

'None of us can reach it,' Robert said.

'We could get a ladder.' Aunt Mary suggested.

'Uh... did you forget that these are heavily guarded?' Emma reminded Aunt Mary.

'Right. We need a distraction.'

'Or... we could ask the guards themselves to do it for us,' Robert said.

'And... how will we convince them to do so? Aunt Mary asked.

'I have an idea,' Robert said. 'We can walk to the guards as innocent tourists and tell them that an important piece of paper flew away and got stuck in the crack.'

'Do you think they'll believe us?' Emma asked.

'Let's just try.' Robert was confident enough.

With their plan in place, the group of adventurers approached the towering limestone guardian. As they neared the rock formation, they could see the guards standing in their silent grace, almost like sentinels of the desert.

Adam initiated the conversation with a friendly wave. 'Hey there! Beautiful day, isn't it?'

The guards, their faces mostly concealed by turbans, nodded in acknowledgment.

Robert chimed in with a smile. 'We're just tourists who couldn't help but admire the beauty of this place. But, you see, there's a little problem.'

Emma nodded along. 'Yes, it's quite embarrassing, really. We were trying to take a picture, and a piece of paper... well, it just flew out of our bag. We think it got stuck in one of those cracks up there.' She pointed to the crevice.

Aunt Mary joined in, adding a touch of urgency. 'That paper means a lot to us. It's a part of our travel journal, and we would greatly appreciate your help in retrieving it. We promise we won't disturb this beautiful place anymore.'

The guards exchanged glances, and after a brief discussion among themselves, one of them stepped forward. He gestured for them to follow him, seemingly understanding the situation.

Emma whispered to Adam, 'I can't believe it worked.'

Aunt Mary gave them a reassuring smile, whispering back, 'Sometimes, honesty is the best approach.'

They led the guard to the crevice where the piece of paper had wedged itself. Using a slender stick, the guard carefully wrought it until the paper came free.

He handed it to Adam, who was immensely grateful. 'Thank you so much! You've been a great help,' Adam said, his voice genuinely appreciative.

The guards nodded. Their silent grace was still undisturbed.

The group thanked them once more and left the limestone guardian, the precious piece of paper now in their possession.

As they rejoined their group, Emma grinned and said, 'Well, that was surprisingly smooth.'

Robert agreed. 'We mustn't underestimate the kindness of strangers, even silent ones.'

The next piece read:

path to myst

ancient won

gold.

With the second piece of the poem in their hands, the group continued their search, determined to find the remaining three limestone guardians and the secrets they held.

The group arrived at the next limestone guardian. Their spirits were high after the successful retrieval of the second piece of the poem. This time, it was Emma's turn to search for the hidden paper.

As they examined the rock formation, Emma couldn't help but notice a pattern etched into the limestone surface. It was like a maze of lines and circles. This sparked her curiosity.

'Hey, guys, come look at this,' Emma called out.

They gathered around her, looking at the mysterious patterns etched into the rock.

'What is it?' Robert asked.

'This looks like a puzzle or something. It's not just random markings. It's intentional.' Emma explained.

Adam examined the patterns, and his interest piqued. 'It does seem puzzling. Maybe it's connected to the location of the hidden paper.'

Aunt Mary nodded. 'I agree. Ancient civilizations often used symbols and patterns to convey messages. This might be a clue to finding the paper.'

They studied the markings, trying to decipher the puzzle. As they traced the lines and examined the circles, Robert noticed something intriguing.

'Look here; these circles seem to align in a certain order, almost like constellations. And these lines... They connect the circles in a specific sequence.'

Emma added excitedly, 'I think we need to follow the lines connecting the circles like a path. It could lead us to the hidden paper.'

The group agreed to give it a try. They began to follow the lines, tracing them with their fingers on the limestone surface, each step taking them deeper into the puzzle.

As they followed the intricate path of lines and circles, they felt a sense of hope, wondering where this mysterious journey would lead them. The ancient puzzle seemed to come to life as they navigated through the patterns.

After a series of twists and turns in their puzzling journey, Emma's finger brushed against a slightly raised part of the limestone.

'I think I found something!' Emma exclaimed.

The others gathered around her as she carefully pried the hidden paper from its concealed spot. They had successfully decoded the intricate puzzle, revealing the third piece of the poem.

This is what the piece of paper contained:

Lies a hidden

In the land of

With just two more pieces left, the group moved on to the next limestone guardian, each eager to decipher the clues and find the next piece of the poem. This time, they saw a carving on the limestone that puzzled them. It depicted a bird gazing intently at a tree.

Aunt Mary examined the carving. 'This carving seems to convey something, but I can't quite figure out its meaning.'

They spent some time discussing the significance of the bird and the tree. Were they symbolic? Was there a hidden message? What do you think?

Robert theorized, 'The bird might represent a location or a landmark, and the tree... could be a reference to something else.'

'It might also have some hidden meaning,' Adam said.

'Wait... Remember that the Egyptian hieroglyphs contained birds?' Aunt Mary suggested that the carving could depict something in Egyptian hieroglyphs.

'Yeah, there are several birds in the Egyptian hieroglyphs, but I don't remember seeing any trees.' Adam said.

Emma, with her sharp observation skills, looked around. The landscape around the limestone formation was vast, and the white desert held a unique beauty. Her eyes caught something intriguing in the distance.

'Wait a minute, guys,' she said excitedly. 'Look over there. Do you see that rock formation?'

They followed her gaze to a distinct rock formation. It indeed resembled a bird, with its head raised as if gazing up at a tree.

A spark of realization swept through the group. 'That's it!' Adam exclaimed. 'The carving on the limestone was a clue pointing us to that rock formation!'

After all the discussions and theorization, it seemed that the solution was not that complicated. Throughout their journey, they encountered several carvings that contained coded information, so they expected it to be something like that. It turns out that easy things can sometimes seem complicated, too.

With renewed excitement, they made their way to the bird-shaped rock formation. As they searched the area, Emma noticed a crevice. She reached into the narrow opening and carefully retrieved the fourth piece of the poem.

The fourth piece read:

tones' shadow, where

ts lie,

azure sky so high,

As the group approached the last limestone formation, they were met with yet another intriguing carving. This time, the stone depicted an ornate archway adorned with intricate details.

Emma, Adam, Robert, and Aunt Mary exchanged knowing glances. They had become skilled interpreters of these ancient symbols, understanding that the carvings held the keys to their next clue.

'This one's clear,' Robert commented. 'We need to find an archway formation that matches this carving.'

Emma, with her eagle eyes, began scanning the horizon. 'I think I see it!' she exclaimed, pointing to a rock formation that indeed resembled the carved archway. It was a natural formation sculpted by the elements over millennia, mirroring the image etched in stone.

The group approached the archway rock formation with a mix of excitement and hope. They were now familiar with the routine–search the crevices for the hidden piece of the poem.

'We know the drill,' Adam said.

'Yeah. Search for more crevices and cracks.' Emma said.

As Adam reached inside one of the crevices within the archway, his fingers brushed against aged parchment. With a glorious smile, he pulled out the next piece.

'Got it!' he announced, carefully unfolding the piece to reveal its contents.

This was the last piece's content:

eries untold,

ders, pure as

'Now that we have all five pieces, let's join them together,' Adam said, eager to reveal the clue.

Emma and Adam, both of whom have uncanny puzzle-solving skills, gathered all the pieces that they found from the five limestone guardians and pieced them together. They revealed a new message:

Beneath the limestones' shadow, where secrets lie,

Underneath the azure sky so high,

Lies a hidden path to mysteries untold,

In the land of ancient wonders, pure as gold.

'Again,' Emma seemed frustrated with something.

'What is it?' Adam asked, curious about Emma's frustration.

'Can't you see? '*Beneath*'. That's what's troubling me.' Emma was frustrated with going underground.

If you have ever been underground, then you'll understand. There is less oxygen for you to breathe, and you'll have a suffocating feeling. Also, it's dark, with torches hardly even lighting up the room. If you have claustrophobia, which is the fear of tight spaces and suffocation, or nyctophobia, which is the fear of the dark, you'll never be able to survive underground.

'Ah, I get it.' Adam understood. 'Even I'm frustrated with going underground again and again'

'Yeah. It's like the ancient civilization couldn't find any place other than underground.' Emma added on.

'I'd say that the one who built the library at Alexandria was a legend.' Adam said.

'You mean 'The Valley of Knowledge', right?' Emma said

'Yeah.'

'Let's just go back to deciphering the poem.' Aunt Mary said. 'We are wasting time'

'There's nothing to decipher,' Adam said as he thought that they just had to go beneath the surface.

'There is.' Aunt Mary said.

'Why? It's clear that there is a "*hidden path to mysteries.*" "*Beneath the limestones' shadow.*"'

'But my question is, what does "*limestones' shadow*" refer to?'

'Hmm... I think you're right. It's not clear which limestone.' Adam realized that the poem was ciphered.

'Also, what does shadow mean? It can't be an actual shadow, can it?' Emma asked.

'It could,' Adam said.

'How? Shadows move. They are not fixed.'

'Maybe the entrance moves too,' Adam said from his previous experiences, as he knew that ancient people were capable of doing anything.

'We're starting to think outside the box, I guess.' Aunt Mary said.

'We have no other option!' Emma exclaimed.

'We do. Think about it. Every single formation is on a dome-shaped base.' Aunt Mary said, pointing at the pedestal-like structure below a limestone formation.

Emma looked at it for a while. 'You mean to say that those are the shadows, right?'

'Yeah'

'Then... which limestone's shadow is it talking about?' Adam asked.

'Read it properly. It's not possessive to *limestone* but to *limestones*.' Aunt Mary said.

'But then, which *limestones' shadows* are the poem talking about?'

'I think it might be the five distinct limestone formations where we found these pieces of paper.' Aunt Mary said, pointing towards the pieces of paper that formed the poem.

'I think you're wrong,' Emma said. Her eyes were focused on something at a distance.

'What is it that you're looking at?' Adam asked Emma.

'If you read the poem carefully, then you'll see that "*limestone*" is in plural, but "*shadow*" is singular.'

'So... you mean that we should look for a limestone formation with one base... but many formations?'

'We don't need to find it. I'm looking at it.' Emma said, still gazing at a distant sight. The rest of them realized that Emma was staring at their key to finding the hidden path.'

With a better understanding of the poem's clues, the group decided to follow Emma's keen observation and head to the limestone formation that seemed to be the key to their next adventure. As they approached it, they couldn't help but marvel at the stunning rock formation. The five distinct limestone guardians stood tall. Their domed bases merged on the ground.

Robert couldn't contain his excitement. 'This is it! The formation we've been looking for.'

Emma nodded with a sparkle in her eyes. 'Yes, this is where the journey continues.'

Adam grinned. 'So, how do we open it? Any ideas?'

Aunt Mary, ever the logical thinker, examined the base of the limestone formation closely. 'There might be some clue in the formation itself.'

'Yeah. Remember how there were carvings in the limestone formations we were investigating before?' Emma said, agreeing with Aunt Mary's point.

Emma's eyes scanned every inch of the intricately carved surface.

'I found something!' Emma said as she saw an etching on the base of the formation.

'Great! What is it?' Adam was curious to know more about Emma's discovery.

'It seems like there's a clue here. See these etchings? They depict not only the limestone formations but also show a certain order.' Emma pointed at the etching she found. All that was etched were arrows, and it looked like this:

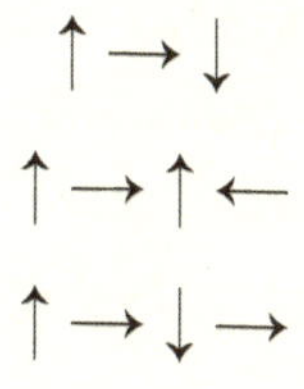

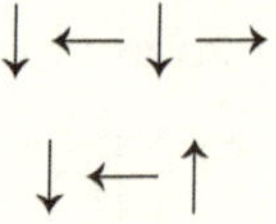

Adam squinted at the etching. 'It's like a set of instructions, but in arrows.'

Adam chimed in, 'It's almost like a puzzle. If only we knew how to solve it.'

Robert, always up for a challenge, contemplated the situation. 'The base, the shadows, the etchings—they're all connected. Maybe we need to move the limestone formations in the order shown in the pattern?'

Aunt Mary agreed. 'It's a plausible theory, but there's a catch. We have a group of guards right there.' She gestured toward the silent guards standing watch.

Emma's eyes widened as she realized the situation. 'We can't just start shifting the rocks while the guards are watching. It's bound to raise suspicion.'

Adam frowned. 'So, how do we create a distraction and shift the limestone formations simultaneously?'

Aunt Mary put on her thinking cap. 'We'll have to be creative. The guards are not easily distracted, and we need to ensure they stay occupied long enough for us to make the move.'

Emma contemplated, 'What can we do? They seem to be focused on their duty.'

Aunt Mary's face brightened with a clever idea. 'What if we arrange something that captures their attention—maybe something that seems even more intriguing than us moving limestone formations?'

Robert was quick to catch on. 'Like a mini-show. Something that would make them turn their heads.'

Emma loved the idea. 'That could work. But what could that show be?'

Aunt Mary chuckled mischievously. 'Well, how about some mesmerizing optical illusion? A trick of the light.'

The group was captivated by Aunt Mary's idea, eagerly awaiting her next move.

Aunt Mary revealed her plan. 'I have a few mirrors in our equipment. We could set them up in such a way that they catch the sunlight and create a stunning light show. We'll position them in such a way that the light dances across the sands, making it seem like an enchanting display. The guards will be too spellbound to notice our actions.'

Adam grinned. 'That's brilliant. I didn't know we were traveling with a magician.'

Emma said with a smile, 'You think the guards will start applauding?'

Robert chuckled. 'Let's hope they do. Now, how do we set this up?'

Aunt Mary distributed the mirrors among the group. 'You'll each need to take a mirror and position it in the sand so that it reflects the sunlight onto the limestone formation. If we angle them just right, the light should create the illusion we need.'

With their mirrors in hand, the group strategically placed them in the sand. As the mirrors caught the sun's rays and began to reflect them onto the limestone formation, a mesmerizing play of light and shadow unfolded.

As the group watched their enchanting show unfold, they couldn't help but admire Aunt Mary's clever plan.

The guards, drawn by the mesmerizing display, turned their attention away from the limestone formations. They were occupied by the shifting patterns of light and shadow, entirely captivated by the optical illusion.

Aunt Mary whispered, 'Now's our chance. Let's move the limestone formations into the order shown in the pattern.'

The group acted quickly and carefully, pushing and turning the limestone formations into the sequence shown by the etchings on the base. As they followed the pattern step by step, the stone guardians seemed to respond as if acknowledging their efforts.

Finally, the limestone formations were placed in the correct order. A sense of anticipation filled the air as the group stood back to admire their work.

'The pattern matches! We did it!' Emma exclaimed.

Robert's eyes sparkled with excitement. 'I can't believe that actually worked!'

Adam beamed with pride. 'I told you Aunt Mary is a magician.'

Aunt Mary smiled, modestly waving off the praise. 'Let's not celebrate too early. This is just the beginning.'

With the limestone formations correctly aligned, the base of the guardian formation began to shift and split apart. A hidden entrance was revealed, leading to a dark and mysterious chamber below.

Chapter 16
The Final Stop

The group eagerly gathered their equipment and prepared to descend into the unknown.

They knew that this was just the first step on a new part of their journey, filled with ancient secrets and untold mysteries. With Aunt Mary's clever plan and their teamwork, they had once again overcome a challenge and were ready to go on the adventure that lay ahead.

With their incredible teamwork and Aunt Mary's clever plan, the group had successfully entered the secret chamber, and their excitement soared as they saw a staircase leading down.

'Great! A staircase.' Adam said that a staircase is something unusual to find, along with a hidden entrance. They had only come across such a scenario once before in their whole journey.

Emma couldn't help but admire the beautiful limestone walls that surrounded them.

'These walls are stunning,' she remarked, running her hand along the smooth surface. 'Can you believe the secrets they've witnessed over the centuries?'

'Yeah. The fact that these walls are made of a material from which chalk is already made makes it seem impossible. It really is unique.' Adam said.

'Just a correction: the walls aren't *made*. This whole chamber is *carved*, and so are the walls.' Robert said.

'Woah! I can't believe all this is carved.' Adam said.

'Argh... Can we admire the walls later?' Aunt Mary, as you know, did not like to talk about things like walls unless they had some secrets. So, eager to explore further, she urged the group to move on.

As they descended deeper into the chamber, their expectancy grew. But as they ventured forward, their path led them to a sudden dead end. The atmosphere took a sad turn, and disappointment filled the air.

Robert sighed in frustration. 'A dead end? Seriously?'

Adam's voice shook with a hint of despair. 'We came all this way for *nothing*?'

Emma, however, wasn't ready to give up just yet. She noticed something unusual on the wall. It was a series of intricate carvings.

'Guys! Come.' She called.

'What is it?' Adam asked. His hopes came back.

'It's a carving.' Emma pointed to a carving that read:

The land where the pyramids stab the sky,

In the realm where pharaohs' treasures hide,

Amidst the scene, your answers unfold,

In the pyramid's heart the next tale is told.

'Great, let me see.' Adam said as he quickly grabbed his notebook and started copying it down.

Adam jotted down the carvings, but before he could even finish, Robert spoke up with a triumphant grin. 'Guys, I've got it! It's a riddle.'

Emma couldn't believe it. 'How did you decode it so fast?'

Robert shrugged. 'I've got a knack for these things. So, this riddle basically tells us our next destination. I think our next destination is the pyramids of Giza.'

Robert continued to copy it down, even though the riddle had already been solved.

Adam couldn't help but tease Robert. 'Why are you writing it down? We already know where we're going.' He said.

Robert laughed. 'I just wanted my own copy. You never know when it'll come in handy.'

With their next destination confirmed as the Pyramids of Giza, the group turned to leave the secret chamber. Their spirits lifted once more. They walked back and ascended the staircase. They emerged to find the guards still utterly engrossed in the mesmerizing light show they had created.

Emma couldn't help but chuckle. 'Those guards are really into our *magic show*. Maybe we missed our calling as illusionists.'

Robert added, 'Who knew we had a secret talent for dazzling desert guards?'

Adam grinned. 'Ha! We're not just adventurers. We're all-around entertainers.'

As they left the limestone formation behind and made their way to the awaiting copter, they couldn't help but admire the breathtaking view of the White Desert. Its stark beauty stretched as far as the eye could see, a stunning contrast to the mysterious secrets they had unearthed.

Aboard the copter, they shared a moment of company, reflecting on the twists and turns of their journey so far.

Robert, with a twinkle in his eye, said, 'Well, that was certainly an unexpected detour.'

Aunt Mary chuckled. 'A detour that led us to yet another chapter of this adventure.'

Emma glanced out the window at the landscape below. 'The world is full of surprises, and we're not even close to finished.'

Adam nodded, his face reflecting a sense of wonder. 'Onward to the Pyramids of Giza, then!'

With their destination set and the taste of new adventure on their lips, they admired the ever-changing panorama of the White Desert as they left it behind. The journey continued, and they were ready to face whatever mysteries the Pyramids had in store.

'Ancient wonders await us!' Emma said, her voice overflowing with enthusiasm.

Robert, who had been deciphering the clues, added, 'The heart of the pyramid may hold the key to unraveling your parents' disappearance.' Wait, how did he know the purpose of their quest? I don't remember anyone telling Robert about their parents' disappearance.

The group, their spirits renewed by the poetic quest, embarked on the next stage of their journey, determined to unlock the mysteries of the Pyramids of Giza and, perhaps, find the answers they had sought for so long.

The group's journey took them to the iconic Pyramids of Giza, a breathtaking sight in the Egyptian desert. Towering against the azure sky, these colossal monuments of ancient engineering left them in awe.

The copter had landed in front of the three Pyramids of Giza.

'They're huge!' Emma exclaimed.

'Right! But which pyramid should we start with?' Adam asked.

'Let's split up,' Robert suggested. Adam, Emma, and Robert each went on to investigate a pyramid. Aunt Mary watched their moves.

Emma went towards the Great Pyramid of Giza and started tapping its walls, hoping to find something hollow. And... she did.

'Guys! I think this is the pyramid that we should search.' Emma said, calling upon the rest of them.

'Really?' Adam said as he walked towards the Great Pyramid of Giza.

'Yeah,' Emma replied with confidence.

'How are you so sure?' Adam asked.

'This seems to be the only one that's hollow,' Emma said. 'And... We know that hollow is what we go for, right?' Emma continued.

'Then... I guess you're right.' Adam understood Emma's theory.

As the others approached the Great Pyramid of Giza, Adam wondered aloud, 'So, how do we find the entrance this time? No cosmic alignments or star patterns here, it seems.’

Aunt Mary asked. ‘What about wishes? Wishes were the way to go to enter the pyramid in The Valley of Knowledge...'

‘No ancient wishes and hieroglyphic codes, too,’ Emma said. ‘I already tried that.'

‘It’s as if the pyramids are playing games with us.’ Adam said.

Aunt Mary suggested, ‘Maybe this time it’s something completely different, something unexpected. We should investigate thoroughly.’

With their spirits high and their curiosity at its peak, they started to explore the area around the Great Pyramid. Emma, with her keen eye, noticed something unusual near the base of the pyramid. It appeared to be a slight depression, unlike the rest of the surface.

‘Guys, come over here! I think I found something,’ she called out.

The group gathered around the spot. Adam examined the depression closely. ‘It’s as if something heavy was resting here, like a stone or a door. But what could it mean?’

Robert, always quick to theorize, suggested, 'Maybe it's an entrance, but it's hidden beneath the sand. We need to uncover it.'

Aunt Mary nodded. 'That's a possibility. Let's dig carefully and see if we can reveal anything.'

With their hands and a few makeshift tools, they began to clear away the sand from the depression. Slowly but surely, a pattern emerged. It was a large circular plate with several intricate markings around the edge.

'What's that?' Aunt Mary asked, starting a conversation.

Emma observed the markings and noticed a minor groove along the edge of the plate. 'It's like a combination lock or a puzzle. Perhaps we need to rotate it in a specific way.'

Adam leaned in closer. 'Look, there are symbols engraved on the plate's surface. Maybe we need to align them somehow.'

Robert cracked a playful smile. 'You know what this reminds me of? Those escape room challenges we used to do back home.'

Aunt Mary joined in the fun. 'Indeed! Only this time, we're in the heart of ancient history, deciphering a puzzle to access hidden secrets.'

With the conversation light and playful, they decided to experiment with the circular plate.

'Maybe we should turn it.' Emma attempted to turn it, but it wouldn't budge. The plate was firmly fixed in place.

Robert examined the symbols more closely. 'I think there's a clue here. Maybe the symbols need to be aligned in a specific order, like a code.'

Aunt Mary encouraged him. 'Let's try different combinations. After all, we have nothing to lose but time, and this is a journey of discovery.'

Hours passed as they patiently rotated and repositioned the circular plate, trying various combinations, laughing at their failures, and celebrating the small successes.

Emma suddenly shouted, 'Guys, look! The symbols are forming a sequence now!'

The rest of the group gathered around, and, with a final twist, the plate clicked into place. The ground trembled beneath them, and the circular plate started to descend into the sand.

The group exchanged wide-eyed glances. 'Did we just find a hidden entrance?' Adam asked, unable to contain his excitement.

They watched as the plate settled into the sand, revealing a dark passageway leading down. Their faces lit up with anticipation as they realized they had unlocked the way into the Great Pyramid of Giza.

'Are we ready for this?' Robert said, his voice filled with excitement.

Emma nodded. 'Absolutely. Let's venture into the heart of the pyramid and uncover the next piece of our adventure.'

With the mystery of the entrance solved in a completely unexpected way, they descended into the Great Pyramid of Giza, eager to uncover the secrets that lay hidden within its ancient stone walls. Their journey continued into the depths of history, with no telling what they might discover next.

The plate was slowly descending, taking all of them slowly into the depths of the pyramid. The plate seemed to take a turn and then slowly ascended. Then, after a while, the plate stopped, and they were inside the pyramid.

'Wow! I never knew that this pyramid was hollow!' Robert said as they entered the pyramid.

'I see.' Aunt Mary said, examining the pyramid.

'There!' Emma said, pointing to a dim source of light, which was precisely in the middle of the pyramid.

'"*In the pyramid's heart the next tale is told.*" That's it. That is what the poem was referring to!' Adam said with excitement.

'Yes, but what is it?' Aunt Mary asked.

Suddenly, a voice spoke, 'I see you do not know what it is.'

'Who was that?' Emma was startled when she heard a new voice... Which was pretty familiar.

'Turn back, and you'll see, my dear.' The voice said.

All of them turned back. It was Cleopatra.

'Cleopatra? What are *you* doing here?' Adam asked, curious about her presence in the pyramid.

'Me? I just came to guide you.' She replied.

'Guide us?' Emma was confused about why they needed her guidance.

'See... Without me, you'll never be able to figure out what it is.' She said, pointing towards the dim source of light.

'Then why don't you tell us what it is?' Emma asked, eager to know the dim light's secrets.

'Right. What you are looking at is not just a source of light. It was a possession of your parents. Your parents found it during a specific research, which you will be continuing. Your parents wanted to keep their discoveries safe and only available to you, so they hid each of their discoveries in a certain place.'

'So, you mean to say that this was in the possession of our parents?' Adam asked.

'Yes, and this is just one. You will have to find many more,' Cleopatra replied.

'But what is its use?'

'Hmm... I don't think I can tell you its exact use. You will have to figure it out on your own.' Cleopatra said. 'But...' she continued, 'I can tell you that this will help you unlock the greatest mystery of all times. No one has ever found it.'

'What do you mean by no one has ever found it?'

'You will know later. Now, you must focus on that.' Cleopatra pointed towards the dim light again.

Emma went closer to the dim light. All she saw was an empty, transparent sphere placed on a dimly glowing pedestal.

'What is this? It's just an empty sphere.'

'Look carefully. Pick it up.' Cleopatra said.

Emma picked it up. She observed it carefully with her keen eyes.

'I see now.' She said.

'What do you see? I don't see anything.' Adam said, still looking at the sphere, which still seemed empty to him.

'It's a grain of sand. Just one tiny little grain of sand. How is it so important?' Emma was curious about how a tiny little grain of sand could be something so great that their parents had to hide it.

'The grain of sand *is* what is important. Not the sphere. The sphere is just a casing that can be opened. It is a protection.' Cleopatra said.

Hearing this, Emma tried opening it, and the tiny little grain of sand turned into a stone. I mean it. The tiny grain of sand, which was barely visible, became a huge... or, let's say, an average-sized stone.

'Wow! That... is a great work of... shrinking,' Adam said, wondering about how their parents were able to shrink an average-sized stone into a tiny grain of sand, which was hardly even visible.

'Yeah! You're right.' Emma wondered the same.

Aunt Mary couldn't help but be amazed at their latest discovery. 'A stone that can change its size? Your parents were truly remarkable researchers.'

'Now that you have the stone, it's up to you to find out its purpose,' Cleopatra said.

'Well and good, but... how do we get outta here?' Adam asked Cleopatra.

'I could help, but you'll feel dizzy after we get out,' Cleopatra said, thinking about teleporting them out, as she had harnessed the power of manipulation after being in the shrine for years.

'Just take us out. Dizzy doesn't matter,' Adam said.

'Right. We have to get out now.' Emma agreed.

And before anyone could say anything else, Cleopatra teleported them out. After their encounter with Cleopatra and the mysterious stone, the group found themselves outside the Great Pyramid of Giza, back in the open air. Luckily, the stone was also teleported along with them.

Emma and Adam were indeed a bit wobbly on their feet, just as Cleopatra had warned them that they might feel a bit dizzy after the teleportation, but the feeling soon passed.

'Where to now?' Aunt Mary asked.

'No idea,' Emma replied, observing the stone.

'I think we should go back to America and investigate this stone.'

'Right. We can't stay here forever. We've already spent one whole year.'

'Yeah... Let's go back to the airport.' Aunt Mary said.

As they reached the airport, they were relieved to find the airplane they had arrived in was still there. They hadn't been sure what to expect, considering it had been left unattended for an entire year.

When they got to the airport, they were like, 'Whoa, our plane's still here?' Seriously, they didn't know what to expect, leaving it alone for a whole year.

Robert, always eager for the next adventure, handed Aunt Mary his contact information and said, 'Mary Wilson, right? Please give me a call when you're ready for your next expedition. I can't resist the temptation of hidden treasures and ancient secrets.'

Aunt Mary chuckled, 'You'll be the first person we call, Robert. Thanks for your help today.'

'Yeah. You have been of great help,' Adam agreed.

Robert bid them farewell as they boarded the plane. It was a nostalgic moment as they waved goodbye to their newfound friend, who had been instrumental in their journey through Egypt.

As the plane's engines roared to life, Adam and Emma took one last look at the ancient land of Egypt from their windows. The pyramids, the Nile, and the vast deserts passed by beneath them. Their hearts were heavy with the knowledge of the mysteries that still lay ahead.

So, with the stone now in their backpack, they hopped on the plane and soared back to America, eager to unravel the mystery left behind by their parents and continue their quest to uncover the greatest mystery of all time.

Their journey was far from over, and the adventures that awaited them would be as extraordinary as the secrets they sought. I mean, come on, they have so much more to discover, and more adventures are waiting for them.

As the plane carried them back home, they couldn't help but wonder what other ancient wonders and hidden treasures they would encounter in the chapters of their continuing adventure.

On the plane ride back home, they were like, 'I wonder what other cool ancient stuff we'll stumble upon in the next part of our adventure!' Seriously, they couldn't stop thinking about all the hidden treasures and mysteries they were gonna find.

Chapter 17
Back to America

Back in America, they finally set foot on home turf.

With a deep sigh, Adam was like, 'Finally! We're back home. That was one great adventure I don't think I'll ever forget.'

'I know you'll forget it. You forget everything.' Emma couldn't help but tease Adam.

'Ha! But now we've got this stone, and I'm dying to know what it's all about.'

Emma was holding the stone, and, in a kind of hopeful tone, she said, 'I wish our parents were here to tell us about this stone.'

And... guess what? Something pretty incredible happened.

The stone started getting carved with some mysterious stuff right there in Emma's hand.

Emma was delighted and turned to Adam. She was like, 'Adam, you won't believe it! The stone is carving something by itself!' She could hardly contain her excitement.

'*What?*'

'Yeah. I'm not lying. Check it out for yourself.'

'Woah!' Adam was all on it, pulling out his notebook.

He jotted down every single detail as fast as his pen could move. Because you know what? The carving started to fade away, but luckily, Adam managed to capture it all on paper just in time.

Once it was all done, they just stared at the carvings, trying to figure out what they could mean. But it was all one big mystery, and they knew they'd have to dig deeper into this one. So, they put the stone aside for now, but you bet it's gonna come back into play in their next adventure.

The next day, Adam embarked on a quest of his own, but it wasn't to uncover ancient mysteries or solve enigmatic riddles. No, he was on a mission to locate his indescribable sister, Emma. He searched for her in their house, turning over cushions and peeking behind curtains like a detective hunting for clues.

However, Emma proved immensely vague during a game of hide and seek. Finally, after an extended hide-and-seek session, Adam decided to consult his inner Sherlock Holmes and widen the search perimeter. He went outdoors. And that's when he spotted her by a scenic lakeside, seemingly engaging in some top-secret operation. She had a handful of pebbles and was launching them into the water with her hands, having all the power of a medieval catapult.

Intrigued and more than a little puzzled, Adam couldn't resist. He waded through the sea of stones strewn across the lakeshore and inquired, 'What brought you to this lakeside?'

Emma's reply was unexpected. 'It's the chess match. I'm still mulling over it. Why do I keep losing to you? You're like the chess champ, and I'm the pawn. I mean, I always lose with you.'

'Emma,' he said softly, realizing why Emma was there. 'I didn't mean to upset you. I understand that losing can be frustrating, especially when it seems like I always win.'

Emma looked up. Her eyes were still filled with annoyance. 'But why do you always win? What's your secret?'

Adam sat down beside her on the bench, watching the gentle ripples in the water. 'It's not really a secret, Emma. It's just years of practice and experience. I've played chess for a long time, and I've learned to think ahead, to anticipate my opponent's moves, and to position my pieces strategically.'

Emma sighed, her frustration starting to dissipate. 'I just feel like I can never catch up. It's discouraging.'

Adam placed a hand on her shoulder, offering support. 'Chess is a game that requires patience and perseverance. It's not something you can master overnight. But if you keep practicing and learning from each game, you'll start to see improvement. It's all about building your own strategies and adapting to different situations.'

Emma looked at him, her expression softer now. 'I guess I just need to be more patient with myself.'

Adam nodded, a reassuring smile on his face. 'Exactly. Rome wasn't built in a day, and becoming a skilled chess player takes time. I believe in you, Emma. You have the potential to be a great player if you don't give up.'

Emma's lips curled into a small smile. 'Thanks, Adam. I appreciate your support.

About the Author

Anish Bhattacharya is a versatile individual whose passions extend across various creative realms. With a deep love for art, music, and playing musical instruments, Anish brings a unique perspective to the world of literature. Alongside these artistic pursuits, Anish is also well-versed in the intricate world of programming and robotics. This multidimensional approach to life is reflected in his work, creating a rich tapestry of creativity and intellect.

www.anish-bhattacharya.in

www.ingramcontent.com/pod-product-compliance
Lightning Source LLC
LaVergne TN
LVHW091300150826
845673LV00006B/1486

* 9 7 9 8 8 9 2 3 3 3 0 9 2 *